Whatever Kills the Pain

C.W. Blackwell

Rock and a Hard Place Press

PRAISE FOR
WHATEVER KILLS THE PAIN

"Blackwell's stories are populated by regular people doing stupid and sometimes terrible things. No one is healed in his stories and the pain these characters carry is rarely dulled for long but I was happy to follow them down their chosen path to bear witness to their end. CW Blackwell is a delightful storyteller. I can't wait to see what else he writes."
—Nikki Dolson, author of *Love and Other Criminal Behavior*

"C.W. Blackwell has a delicate touch with hard stories and an uncommon knack for bringing them in hot. You'll walk away from *Whatever Kills the Pain* heart-bruised and relishing the ache."
—Wes Browne, author of *They All Fall the Same*

"With every story, C.W. Blackwell creates worlds. Worlds of desperation, dead ends, anger, and blood. And worlds of pathos, of humans being human, of life eating souls. *Whatever Kills the Pain* is a tremendous read."
—Coy Hall, author of *A Séance for Wicked King Death* and *The Switchblade Svengali*

"C.W. Blackwell's achingly real characters battle back against
the tide of a world seemingly determined to drown them all,
struggling to find slivers of hope and redemption. WHATEV-
ER KILLS THE PAIN pulses with both empathy and rage,
shining a light into the encroaching darkness and daring you
to look away. Blackwell's stories will move you and shake you,
they will make you angry, and they will stay with you long after
you've turned the last page. This is a collection by a writer at
absolutely the top of his game."
—James D.F. Hannah, Shamus-winning author of *Behind the
Wall of Sleep* and *Because the Night*

"Stories that sing with love. Love for flawed characters, love
for messed up places where people get stuck, and love for writing
about them, with a spoonful of hope and an occasional dash of
humor. Because nobody is truly thoroughly bad, just human
and inclined to make bad decisions, or often being forced into
making them by others and a world that doesn't care. C.W.
Blackwell's stories grab you by the scruff of the neck and demand complete attention, full emotional involvement. "Whatever Kills the Pain" is that rare collection where stories build
upon one another, exploring different tones and moods, like
these color swatches that take you through the rainbow so slowly and smoothly that you remain unaware of the breathtaking
journey. Just leaving you slightly dazed by all the beauty at the
end."
—M.E. Proctor, author *Love You Till Tuesday* and *Catch Me on
a Blue Day*

For everyone who has been overlooked, knocked down, written off, kicked to the curb, robbed of dignity, tormented by vengeful ghosts, or nurtured by the fire of a burning rage, Whatever Kills the Pain *is for you . . .*

Contents

Introduction

If you're reading this, there's a small chance I am dead.

That's not so bad—most of the authors on your bookshelf are dead, so I am in very good company. What you may want to know is—*how did I die?* As a citizen of the wealthiest state in the wealthiest country in history, you may think I died a wrinkled centenarian with world-class palliative care. But the statistics are against me—and against us all. Because the astonishing truth is that, despite GDP reaching *thirty trillion dollars* by the end of 2024, the U.S. has the worst health outcomes in the industrialized world. Statistically, we're far more likely to die from common preventable diseases than our counterparts in the OECD, and the gap is widening. But wait—in addition to poor health outcomes, the U.S. also has the largest prison population in the world, doesn't it? So maybe I died in prison, taking a toothbrush shiv to the throat. And I'd be relatively young, too, since the U.S. ranks 60th in the world for life expectancy—with the highest suicide rate among wealthy nations, perhaps due to having the highest levels of personal credit card debt.

Will I die early, unhealthy, incarcerated, indebted, by suicide?

Did I mention gun violence? How could I forget the gun violence?

Jesus Christ, the gun violence!

As Americans, we're told from a young age that we will grow up to be whatever we want to be. If we simply work hard and play by the rules, we'll enjoy unimaginable economic mobility. This may have been true for some people, at some point in American history, under certain limited conditions. But today, thirty-eight million Americans can't afford basic necessities, according to recent government figures. It's not for me to say why, only that it is so. Perhaps we can blame fifty years of trickle-down economics, which has sucked fifty trillion dollars from the bottom ninety percent of income-earners and redistributed it to the wealthiest ten percent—a reverse Robin Hood effect of apocalyptic proportions.

So maybe by the time you read this, I will have died the way many of my fellow Americans have died before me: chasing the fabled American dream through never-ending fields of barbed wire. And that's just how my characters die—environmental refugees with poison in their bellies; victims of wage theft who are desperate to risk it all; families under the cruel heels of abusive landlords. All of them hanging from capitalism's meat hooks in a system designed to benefit the upper crust alone. They die because the game is rigged, and we're forced to play whether we want to or not. They die because there are no second chances. They die because despite our charming fairy tales about self-made millionaires and golden ladders to climb, there's a fat man in a tailored suit waiting at the top with his monogrammed shoe on that final rung, eager to kick us into the gutter. And brother, sometimes climbing from the gutter is as likely as climbing from your own grave.

I hope you enjoy these heartfelt stories of courage and desperation.

C.W. Blackwell
November 2024
Santa Cruz, California

"There's more beauty in truth, even if it is dread-ful beauty."

———John Steinbeck

"Desperation is the raw material of drastic change."

—William S. Burroughs

"Isn't it a pity . . . the wrong people always have money."

—The Big Clock, 1948

Hard Rain on Beach Street

July, 1978

"If I hear that song one more time, I'm gonna shoot someone," says Danny.

He sucks his inhaler and watches a white Camaro motor through the parking lot, a Bee Gees tune cranked so loud you can hear the fenders rattle. The Camaro's packed tight with sunburned teenagers belting lyrics with their arms dancing out the windows, hands snaking the warm night air. A clown car of tube tops and hairspray. They hook left onto Beach Street and Danny follows the car with his eyes.

"You're watching the wrong car," I tell him. I tap the wristwatch hanging from the rearview mirror. "Stay focused on the Oldsmobile. Should be five minutes, now."

Danny flicks on the radio. Some rock station from the college. I flick it off again.

"Eyes up," I say. "This is important."

The Oldsmobile idles beside the main ticket booth, below the tall, twisting track rails of the Giant Dipper. We listen to the roar and clatter of the rollercoaster, screams pitching and fading as ridecars swoop around the bend and dip out of sight. We've only ridden the Giant Dipper once since we came to town. Neither of us admitted it was scary, even though you could see the fear in Danny's eyes when we took the first big drop. He's been that way since we were kids—a tough-talking guy with eyes that say otherwise. I never tease him for acting so tough. When you grow up as sick as he did, you do what you can to keep the bullies at bay.

At eleven-fifteen, a bald man slips out of the ticket booth with a blue duffle over his shoulder and knocks on the Oldsmobile's trunk. When the lid latch releases, he sets the duffle inside, closes the trunk lid, and climbs into the backseat. The car idles for a minute longer before easing across the walkway and onto the road.

I flick on the headlights, wheel off the curb, and follow.

It's almost never muggy on the Central Coast, but tonight it is. The streetlights hang in orange halos over the river. I can feel the sweat beading on my forehead. It feels good to be moving with the windows down, even though the air smells bad. The locals have been talking about it all week—a school of sardines got trapped in the harbor and went belly-up, bringing a frenzy of seabirds and foul air. You couldn't escape it if you tried.

"Now can we listen to the radio?" says Danny. He's got the dial pinched between his fingers, watching me like I'm the pain in the ass. It's the same look he's given me since he learned how to give looks.

"No," I say. "I need to concentrate."

"That's the problem. Your nose whistles when you concentrate. I'm tired of hearing it."

"Look who's talking, wheezy." I plug a nostril and blow my nose out the window. "It's this goddamn stink in the air. It's affecting my sinuses."

"The radio'll take your mind off it."

He sucks his inhaler and doesn't take his eyes off me.

"Fine," I say. "Just keep it low."

The college station comes on again. This time it's a Zeppelin tune. Louder than I'd like, but I'm no longer in a fighting mood. I follow the Oldsmobile across the San Lorenzo River, left on Laurel, right on Front Street. There's plenty of cars on the road, traffic backing up at the intersections. Mostly kids headed home from the amusement park. At the Bank of America on River Street, the Oldsmobile slows and wheels into the parking lot, then it loops around and parks facing the street.

I pull next to a shuttered taqueria and we watch from the shadows.

The driver steps out. A tall man with a neatly-trimmed mustache—the kind you see on TV cop shows. Danny calls him a *rent-a-cop*. He's plainly dressed, but he doesn't wear the clothes well. Like he's trying too hard to blend in. He circles the bank on foot, taking his time, spinning the car keys on his finger as he goes. When he reappears from the back of the building, he unlocks the trunk, moves to the night drop window and gives a signal to the bald man.

"That's your cue, baldy," says Danny.

I shush him, but he's right about the timing. The bald man exits, retrieves the blue duffle from the trunk, and makes his way to the bank drop box—the tall man standing watch all the while.

"I say three bags tonight," says Danny.

"I say four easy."

"No way. A dollar says three."

We shake on it.

The bald man unzips the duffle and removes a plastic deposit bag with black scrawl on the outside—account numbers and other bank info. The bag is fat with cash, a green tick ready to pop. The drop box groans as he tilts it open and shoves the bag into the slot, then another. We watch intently and count five bags.

Danny whistles.

"Tomorrow there'll be more," I say. "America's birthday, but me and you will get all the presents."

Danny opens the glove box and regards the leather slapjack and loaded .38 resting inside. He pretends to pull out the revolver, makes a shape of a gun with his hand instead. He cocks his thumb and bends it twice.

"Bang bang," he says.

He blows the phantom gun smoke from the tips of his fingers with a wheeze and a cough.

"Bang bang, little brother," I say.

***

We came out West after the Hooker Chemical Company dumped twenty-thousand tons of poison into our water supply.

Before that, we had it pretty good.

Pop was a union plumber, Local 22. He rode the post-war boom straight into a three-bedroom house in a new neighborhood called Love Canal, with a wife and kids and a shiny blue Chevy sedan in the garage. Mom was a librarian at the high school and hustled Avon on the side. I played little league and rode a paper route for the Niagara Gazette. It was heaven until it was hell. The stench off the canal drove us all indoors, the water oozed black. Mom passed before we even knew she was sick, and Danny hasn't taken an easy breath since his fifth birthday.

So we quit Love Canal for the clean ocean breezes of California.

But the damn poison followed us.

It followed Pop, anyway.

"Heads up," says Danny, nodding with his inhaler aloft. He takes a noisy hit and gestures out the window as we're turning onto our street. There's a blue and white strobe popping against the apartment buildings.

We both know it's not for us. It can't be.

"I bet you Pop's up to his old tricks," I say.

It's a good guess. I pull to the curb and spot the old man as soon as I step out of the car. He's standing in the neighbor lady's front yard in his tighty-whities, waving his arms and demanding that Richard Nixon come out. Thing is, our father just calls him Dick, and there's no blaming an old woman for calling the cops on a half-naked man who's dancing on her lawn and screaming about Dick.

The city cop sees us coming. He's a middle-aged man with a gray mustache and black hair coming out his ears. He's relieved, and it makes his hard brown eyes look friendly.

"This your father?" he says. He's got his arms stretched out in front of him like he's about to wrestle the old man to the ground.

"Yeah," I say. "Just a touch of the Old Timer's. We'll keep a better eye on him next time."

The cop lifts his hat and wipes the sweat from his forehead. He gives a stern look, warning us with his eyes. Then he throws a nod to the neighbor, who's watching from her kitchen window, a cup of tea in her hand. Big round curlers in her hair. I give an apologetic wave, but the curtains shut quickly and that's the end of it.

I slip off my jacket and wrap it around the old man's shoulders and guide him across the street, back to our low-rent two-bedroom apartment.

"Come on, Pop," I say, "Jimmy Carter's on the telephone."

Danny shoots me a dirty look, shakes his head. He doesn't like when I poke fun at Pop. Their relationship always had a softer touch, something sweeter between the lines. I try not to take it personally and chock it up to him being the baby of the family—*the meatball*, as our mother called it.

Danny takes the old man by the elbow.

"Let's go, Pop," he says. "I'll fix you a drink and put you to bed."

"When's Mom gonna be here?" asks Pop. "It's getting late."

"She's on an airplane," says Danny, without missing a beat. It's his standard reply, and it always works. "Probably looking down on us right now and waving."

The old man tilts his head and squints into the fogged-out sky as if he might catch a glimpse of her passing overhead.

***

Next day, I go to the hardware store and buy a second deadbolt for the front door, and I install it so the thumb latch is on the outside. Just something to keep Pop from bothering the neighbors while Danny and I take care of what needs taking care of. It isn't something I'd mention to the landlady, and certainly not the Fire Chief—but it's temporary. I keep reminding myself this whole town is temporary. Just a pitstop on our way down the coast where an armful of amusement park cash will stretch far.

The air is stifling, worse than yesterday. And by the smell of it, the sardines in the harbor still have a collective death wish. It almost reminds me of the summers back home—although I'd take the smell of dead sardines over whatever Hooker Chemical was cooking up any day.

We park in the same place, watching the rollercoaster rise and fall. Rock-O-Planes wheeling at the dark sky. The teenagers are all dressed in stars and stripes, waving sparklers and lighting bottle rockets on the beach. Girls spin in the street with hot pink roller skates, laughing and twirling—maybe a little drunk, a little high. Maybe it's the joy of youth. I can tell Danny wants to go talk to them, and I wish he could. He wants to be a teenager on a hot summer night, too. But I've got to keep him focused.

"No radio tonight," I say. "So don't ask."

I sense Danny rolling his eyes in my periphery.

"When we get where we're going, I'm buying my own radio," he says. "I'm gonna listen to whatever I want. *Whenever I want.* Zeppelin, Sabbath, whatever."

"That so?"

"Oh yeah. I'm gonna answer every DJ trivia question and win a truckload of concert tickets. I'll take a different girl to each concert."

"I won't stop you, big guy."

"What are you gonna do with the money?"

"I'm gonna buy headphones so I don't have to hear all the caterwauling on your new radio."

Sometime before midnight, I spot lightning forking over the bay. Soon, there's more of it. They call the ridecars in, and a few minutes later, a hard rain starts to fall. Everyone comes running out of the amusement park, laughing and shouting. Nobody's brought an umbrella. Some are gathering under the blue and red eves of the carousel. A blonde slips in the street and her friends stop to help her up. Danny rolls his window down and sticks out his palm just to watch it get wet.

"I didn't think it was supposed to rain here," he says.

"It's not. Not in the summertime."

"Maybe we brought the New York weather with us?"

I tap Danny's leg and point out the windshield.

The bald man is rushing from the ticket booth with the blue duffle held low. It looks heavy. The Oldsmobile is waiting for him, tailpipes gently smoking. In all the excitement, neither of us saw it pull up. He lumbers over the open trunk and dumps the duffle inside. Then he shuts the lid—nearly slipping as he opens the rear door, scrambling into the back seat.

I start the car and put it in gear.

We follow close behind, closer than I'd planned. I figure the driver's paying more attention to the weather conditions than who might be following. Besides, the car windows are gelled with rainwater. It's like we're driving through the surf at high tide—all I can see is the red glow of the taillights and a vague Oldsmobile-like shape ahead of us as we forge the slick and steamy streets toward downtown.

By the time we reach the Bank of America on River Street, the downpour has lightened to a steady, easy rain. I stop the car on the Water Street Bridge and let Danny cross on foot, just like we'd rehearsed. He dons a plastic Uncle Sam mask and gives me a salute with his black leather slapjack as if to say *I WANT YOU*, and then he hustles down into the alley behind the bank. I continue on behind the taqueria and park there, watching as the Oldsmobile circles the bank lot and comes to a stop facing the street. The timing is perfect. The rent-a-cop with the thin mustache exits the driver door with a folded newspaper over his head. He glances around the parking lot and starts along the side of the building to walk his perimeter, only this time he's hustling to avoid the rain.

I take the .38 from the glove box and check the cylinder, slip on my own Uncle Sam mask. A lone car passes, tires hissing on the wet road. I watch it veer left over the bridge and disappear in all the static.

"Come on, big guy." I whisper, dancing my fingers on the steering wheel. "Just like we practiced. Two or three hard whacks."

It takes Danny longer than it should.

When he finally pops out from behind the bank, he's stumbling in the parking lot, holding his gut. My own stomach tightens. He looks like he's been shot, but I know that can't be true. I would have heard it. Baldy would have heard it, too—as far as I can tell, he's status quo in the back of the Oldsmobile.

Danny raises one hand over his head and dangles the car keys, and I hurry across the street, gun in my waistband. He gives me a thumbs up with his other hand like everything's fine, but I can tell he's hurt. I can hear his breath over the sound of the rain. Gasping, wheezing. But I take the thumbs-up at face value and continue with the plan. I throw open the driver's door and level the .38 on the headrest so it's pointed at the bald man.

He watches me with hateful little eyes.

"We saw you following us," he says. If his eyes looked hateful, his voice was absolutely loathsome. "Down on Beach Street. We almost changed things up."

"Don't be so hard on yourself," I say. Danny has the trunk open, and maybe it's my imagination, but I can feel the Oldsmobile rise up a little when he lifts the duffle. "I want you to lay down in the back seat and count to three hundred. You understand?"

"Yeah, I get it."

"Good. Now we both have something in common."

"What could we possibly have in common?"

"We'll both be doing a lot of counting tonight."

Again with those wicked eyes.

Danny shuts the trunk and knocks twice, and I flick the gun at baldy, who reluctantly curls up on his side and closes his eyes. There's something infantile about it, like he's waiting for us to leave so he can suck his thumb or sing himself a lullaby.

"Three hundred," I say, and I'm about to shut the car door when I stop and tell him: "Do yourself a favor and hire an armored car."

I take the car keys from Danny and hurl them onto the roof of the building, then I shoulder into the duffle and we start across the street toward the car. I've got one arm around Danny—he's leaning into me hard, feet shuffling on the asphalt as he goes. He finds the inhaler in his jacket pocket and draws a hit as we near the car and climb in. I'm about to ask what happened when someone starts shouting.

"Oh God," says Danny, coughing and pointing. "He's coming."

I look.

The rent-a-cop comes staggering along the side of the bank, face bloody, jacket off. He looks like a car wreck survivor, like someone trying to flag down a ride to the hospital. His shirt is torn, and one pant leg hangs in ribbons. He yells again, but I'm too busy getting the car started to make out what he's saying.

"Hurry," says Danny. "He's got a gun."

A shot rings out and a spark dances across the hood of the car.

A spiderweb blooms in the windshield.

I drop the car into reverse, and we go backward down a dark, lampless one-way street. Another shot—*and another*. It sounds like he's wasting bullets now, firing blindly, angrily. When the road tees off with Pacific Avenue, I hook the car a little too hard and we spin a quarter turn over the slick asphalt. The car stalls, but it's nothing fatal. The ignition kicks right back up, and a moment later, we're zipping through downtown streets toward our little apartment on Blackburn.

"What the hell happened in the alley?" I say.

Danny holds his gut with one hand, the inhaler with the other.

"I couldn't knock him out," he says. "I must have hit him eight times with that silly stick. He hit me, too—knocked the wind out of me." He doubles over as if his stomach suddenly recalled the blow. "Man, it just turned into a wrestling match."

"Why were his clothes torn up?"

Danny scrubs his face with his hands. He looks haunted.

"I gave him a really hard whack and it finally stunned him. He didn't pass out, just sort of had a dopey look on his face. Then I dragged him to the levee and rolled him into the river."

"Into the river?"

"Yeah, straight down into the river scrub. I didn't know what else to do with him. That was one tough son of a bitch, I tell you. He kept grabbing at his ankle, and now I know why. He had a piece down there. *He could've shot me.*" But there's something else, now—a little curl at the corner of his mouth that could be a smile.

"All right, what's that look for?"

His smile broadens into something sweet and childlike.

"I looked in the duffle," he says.

"Oh yeah?"

"Yeah." He holds up four fingers on each hand.

"Eight bags?"

"Eight bags."

"Goddamn," I say. "We're practically rich. What a haul."

***

Police lights erupt on Laurel Street, just a block from home.

A single cop car, parked ahead of us on the side of the road.

This time it could be for us, and we both know it.

I tuck the .38 under my thigh as we draw near. All I want to do is flip a U-turn and haul ass the other direction, but it's too late to turn around without drawing suspicion.

"Try not to look like you just got your ass kicked," I tell Danny.

He sits up straight, folds his hands in his lap.

"What if it's Pop again?"

I'm about to tell him it's impossible, the reverse deadbolt is foolproof.

But then I see him.

Pop is sprawled on the road shoulder, looking up at the sky, working his arms and legs as if making some kind of crude, urban snow angel. This time, at least, he's clothed—but the clothes are soaked through and his hair is drenched and filthy. I can't tell if he's injured or just caught in the webs of his disease. Danny jumps out of the car before I can pull over. He runs to Pop and kneels in the gutter, hands all over his face, trying to get a good look at him. I place the revolver under the seat and hurry over. I spot the city cop talking on the police radio—it's the same cop as last night with the gray mustache. He cradles the receiver when he sees me, straightens his uniform, and heads towards us.

"An ambulance is on the way," he says, coldly.

It's stopped raining now, just a slight drizzle, and there's a sour smell of pitch coming off the road. I ask what's happened to Pop, but Danny already has the old man sitting up, looking him over. He doesn't look hurt, just confused. Body shaking. I take off my jacket and shoulder it over Pop, and he looks at me unknowingly, like I'm just a good Samaritan. He thanks me with a small, frail voice.

"No need for the ambulance," I tell the cop. "We'll get him home and warm him up."

"He'll have to go to the hospital," he says. "You had your warning, pal. This time I'm writing it up."

"Really—" I try to insist, but the cop won't have it.

"He could have died out here," he says. "He's hypothermic. Whatever you're doing isn't good for anyone."

"He'll be fine."

"Look at him. He could have caused an accident out here, lying in the street."

Danny's already walking the old man to the car.

"Hear me out," I say. I'm trying to stall and trying to hurry at the same time. I know once Danny gets the old man into the car with the heater cranked up, we'll be home free. He's not going to pull us all out of the car again. And we desperately need to get off the road. "We've got a live-in nurse starting next week. It's the last time, I promise you."

"A live-in nurse?"

"That's right."

The cop's blood pressure is rising. I can see it the way his hard eyes glower, the way his jaw tightens—and that's when the chatter comes over the radio. It's loud and urgent and bureaucratic. The dispatcher yells out call signs and locations, giving a litany of code violations. Other cops respond with their own call signs, barking their locations, sirens howling in the background.

It's the kind of chatter that might fit a couple of guys like us.

A couple of guys who just did what we did.

I let him worry about the radio and ease back to the car. Danny's already got the old man in the passenger seat with the heater cranked up. All I've got to do is duck behind the wheel and spin off into the night. Forget the apartment, all the junk and trouble we brought from our old life. All that matters is the three of us and the mountain of cash in the trunk.

"Hold up," says the cop.

His whole demeanor shifts from agitation to a keen, deadly interest. He's got his thumb on his duty weapon, giving our car a heavy dose of eyeball. The cracked windshield. The bullet hole in the hood. He peers through the windows to get a better look at Danny, who's still fiddling with the heater from the back seat.

I stop, slowly turn around.

"Where were you both tonight?" says the cop.

The radio is giving descriptions of two young men.

"Nowhere. Just watching the fireworks."

"Nowhere isn't a place."

The cop unclasps the radio and announces his location.

Laurel and Blackburn.

Two young males and an elderly man in a Ford LTD.

Code three backup.

I hear a siren down the street. Maybe four blocks, maybe closer. It could be the ambulance, but I can't be certain. What I know is that any second, they'll ID us all—and that big blue duffle will be laid out on the hood along with the next ten or fifteen years of our lives.

Gunshot.

The cop reels back against the trunk of the police car.

Danny stands by the rear passenger door of the LTD with the .38 in his hands, and now the sour smell of pitch coming off the road is mixed with gunsmoke. I scramble for the driver door, but the city cop's not finished. He fires back—one hand grasping his bloody gut, the other squeezing off rounds at the car. Danny ducks into the backseat as the windshield whitens and glass chimes over the dash. I put my foot into the pedal and make a skirling U-turn in a cloud of heavy white smoke.

***

Something's not right.

Danny's trying to tell me something, but I can't hear what he's saying over Pop's urgent questions. The rear door is ajar, swinging loose in the night air. Danny's writhing against the seat with his hand clasped over his neck and the sounds he's making aren't anything an inhaler can fix. I ask him if he's hit, ask him three or four times as I take the turns, zagging through downtown streets, praying that each turn I take isn't full of blue and white lights. Across the bridge, another hard left on

Dakota. The rear door slams shut with the force of the turn. I cut the lights and weave through San Lorenzo Park and stop the car between two humongous redwood trees. The park is dark and quiet, but police sirens haunt the rest of the city—maybe sirens always sound haunted when they're screaming your name in the dark.

Danny isn't trying to talk anymore.

I flick on the dome light.

The cream-colored seats are painted red.

I climb back and try to sit him up, but it's no use. I'm sobbing, telling him it's going to be okay even though it's a lie. I tell him it's not so bad. Pop is crying, too. Danny's hand falls by his side and his eyes fix on something far away, something I can't see. He's staring through the roof of the car and up into the crowns of the redwood trees. There's a grisly bullet wound in his neck and it's still weeping blood even though I know by now his heart has stopped.

***

We leave the LTD in the park and set Danny up on a bench so he's facing south toward the bay, where fireworks are still blooming over the old amusement park. I leave the key in the ignition, the radio tuned to the college station. Pop and I choke out goodbyes while the music plays, both of us sick with grief. I hope for his sake they don't play the Bee Gees, but I know it doesn't really matter.

The river is low, and we walk along the scrub in the dark. I spot a dead coyote bloating in the moonlight. Fish carcasses with their eyes rotted out. I've got the duffle slung over my shoulder, and one hand on Pop's back, guiding him along. He's quiet, and that means he's lucid, even though I wish he wasn't.

"We're just going to leave him there, huh?" he says, looking back over his shoulder, wiping his wet eyes with his arm. "Just leave him for dead?"

"Yea, Pop," I say. "We have to leave him. He's already gone."

"I'm not too old to carry him," he says. "I'm strong enough."

"I know you are, Pop. It has to be this way."

"Where are we going?"

"South. Maybe San Diego."

"Why?"

"Because things didn't go as we planned."

We quit the river and hike up to a dirt overlook where I spot a white Chevy coupe sitting under a cypress tree. Inside, there's a couple fooling around, radio loud, suspension groaning. They're listening to the college station and my first thought is I wish it were Danny inside, making out with one of those girls from the amusement park, her tube top and hot pink roller skates scattered over the back seat. I rap my knuckle on the foggy window and tell them to open up in my best cop voice.

The door creaks open and a naked young man peers out.

He sees the gun and his eyes clock wide.

Danny's blood is all over my clothes.

"It's all right," I say. "Get dressed. We just need the car."

Ten minutes later, we're on the highway heading south. Pop starts humming and I know he's checked out again—and for once, I'm jealous. I wish I could check out, too. The harbor is close by, and the smell of dead sardines pours through the heater vents. Pop notices it, and the stench seems to bring him back to center.

"This town's gone bad," he says, wrinkling his nose. "Time to pack up and go where the air is cleaner."

"Yeah, Pop. That's a good idea. We're driving out now."

"To California?"

"We're in California, heading south now. We'll start a new life."

He peers into the empty backseat.

"What about Mom and the boy?"

"They're taking a plane," I say—and I'm quick, too. *Just like Danny would have been.* "Probably looking down on us right now and waving. We'll meet them at the airport."

The old man gazes thoughtfully out the window. It's clearing now, stars marbled around the tattered gray clouds. There's an airplane passing low, wingtips blinking, maybe watching the last of the fireworks extinguishing along the edge of the continent. I can still see faint bursts coming and going, lighting up the sky, and I wonder how many families like ours came out west to escape the slow demise of the American dream, only to find it dying everywhere else, too.

"You know, by god, I think I see them," says Pop, waving.

A Little Rain Must Fall

"*This is so fucked*," thought Mirabel as she inched through the rotten access door, gripping her left hand to quell the bleeding. She wasn't worried about the slice on her finger as much as the four-hundred-dollar pipe cutter that had busted apart in her hands—a four-hundred-dollar pipe cutter that had become a six-hundred-dollar debt over the last eighteen months of minimum payments and interest charges.

Raoul watched her crawl from under the house into the cool December light with her jumpsuit caked with mud, a grotesque black smear running from her cheekbone clear down her neck. He didn't offer to help her to her feet.

"You're bleeding," was all he said.

She sat up, watched him back.

"That's your expert opinion?"

"Your hand is bleeding," he clarified. "You should get a Band-Aid or something."

"Or something," she said.

She rinsed the cut under a rusty garden faucet and dressed it with gauze and tape from the first aid kit in the work truck. Whatever she was going to make from the job was now going straight back into tools, and a part of her just wanted to forget it all and jump into the ocean and drown. Or maybe instead of drowning, she'd swim all the way across the Pacific and start a new life as a deckhand on a squid boat. Anything but this.

She noticed the blinds stir in the windows, a pair of eyes leering from the dark *V* it made as a finger bent the slats and released them. The house was a plain tract home with a lava rock yard and dead rose bushes in the planter boxes. Someone had pried the address numbers from the front door, but the phantom outlines remained—a numerical woodstain that read 1-1-8. It was the kind of house everyone skipped on Halloween. Something close to blight, and perhaps one community meeting away from having the windows boarded with plywood. Parked along the curb, a silver BMW sat idling, a middle-aged driver glancing up from a paperback novel to monitor them as they worked.

"These customers are strange," said Mirabel. "Feels like we're under surveillance."

Raoul was about to respond when his cell phone rang. He held out a finger, demanding silence.

"Yes?" he said. "No, no problems at all, sir. Yes, I understand. Shouldn't be too long now. Oh, that's very generous of you, sir."

"I take it that's them?" She could hear the conversation through the speakerphone but was too busy with her bandage to pay any attention.

Raoul hung up, glanced at the BMW.

The driver still had the phone to his ear.

"He says they'll pay us extra if we skip our lunch and pick up the pace."

"You forgot to tell them about the busted pipe cutter."

"What busted—? *Oh dammit, Mirabel.*"

"It snapped in my hands," she said, gesturing at the crawl-space. "Never happened before. Almost lost a finger over it, so I'm not exactly thrilled either."

Raoul was trying not to signal anything was wrong. He had his fingers tucked in his armpits with a phony smile stretched wide. He toed at a weed in the driveway as if everything was perfectly right with the world.

"Shit. All right—you can use mine. But if you break it, I'm not paying you today. Understand? These things are very expensive, you know. You're supposed to provide your own tools, and you damn well know that's part of the gig." He went to the back of the truck and dug out another pipe cutter and presented it to her the way a jeweler might display a diamond necklace. "Are you still bleeding, or do you need another minute?"

"I'll be fine."

"Good," he said. "Now get back under that house and cut the goddamn pipe."

***

When she returned home, the apartment was dark, and she thought at first Tracy was working late again. She heard soft cries coming from the bedroom, the sound of a pill bottle rattling. A faint blue glow from the TV in the corner. Tracy was sitting in bed with a glass of wine at her lips and a box of tissues in her lap. She glanced up in the dark and gave a tiny shrug like she knew she was a mess and nothing could be done about it.

"What's wrong, sad girl?" said Mirabel. She wandered into the room, trying not to touch anything with her muddy clothes. She'd peeled off her jumpsuit and work boots and left it all in the carport, but some of the work grime had seeped through to her jeans. "Vance being a little bitch again?"

"Vance wasn't at work today," she said. There was a distance in her voice that could have come from the pills, the depression, or both. "But everyone else was shittier than usual to make up for it. Even the regulars." She noticed the bandage on Mirabel's finger and reached across the bedside table to flick the light on. She gently drew her hand near to inspect it. "Oh no—what happened? Is it bad?"

"Not as bad as it looks," she said. "Broke my pipe cutter though. Lucky I didn't lose a finger."

"Didn't you just buy one of those?"

"They don't make them like they used to, I guess." Mirabel plucked the pill bottle from the table and looked it over. "Going through these pretty fast, babe. What are you gonna do if you get ahead of your refills?"

"Curl up and die, that's what."

"Don't say that."

"Curl up and wish I was dead, then."

"That's not any better," said Mirabel. "I don't like when you talk like that."

"You don't like when I talk at all."

"That's not even close to true."

"It feels true."

"Well, not to me it doesn't. So, I guess we just cancel out, right?"

Tracy flipped a hand in the air like an old French actress.

"Great," she said. "I always dreamed of someone canceling me out."

Mirabel set the pills on the table and went to the little kitchenette to refill the glass with cold tap water. She preheated the oven and pulled a box of frozen taquitos from the freezer. There wasn't much that cheered Tracy up these days, but sometimes taquitos worked. And wine. With the pills, the wine just as often made her pass out—but she always said that being unconscious had its benefits. Whatever beat-down, dead-inside malaise Tracy was feeling, Mirabel was beginning to feel too. Although she couldn't tell whether it was stemming from their relationship, the rental market, or the mere act of being born into a slog of a world she never consented to inhabit.

"I'm taking a quick shower," called Mirabel. "Oven's heating up for taquitos." When Tracy didn't answer, she peered into the bedroom and found her asleep, tucked into her pillow. Tiny snores like the sound of torn paper. She brought the glass of water and set it on the table beside her. The TV was playing some reality show from a generation ago and a rich-looking older woman with big curly hair was complaining about some other woman's breast implants. "Trace, baby you gotta eat something."

Tracy mumbled and curled tighter into a ball.

"Trace, I'm worried about us," said Mirabel, tucking the blanket around her. She whisked a strand of blond hair behind her ear and kissed her forehead. "We hardly talk anymore."

***

She was getting out of the shower when she noticed a missed call from Raoul. Then a text came through—and another right behind it.

WHERE'S MY PIPE CUTTER? NOT WITH TOOLS

She hammered a quick reply: I DON'T HAVE IT

The little dots scrolled over the text field and she stood naked with the phone in her hand, waiting for the reply. She thought she knew where it was but didn't want to be the one to mention it first.

GO BACK TO HOUSE ON OCEAN ST. NEED IT FOR EARLY JOB.

Fuck.

NO CAR. PICK ME UP?

YOUR FAULT. YOU DEAL WITH IT. ASAP.

She poked several replies into the text field but erased them all. Each of them would've gotten her fired—and one response was probably a misdemeanor. It was ten blocks to the job site and she was hungry, tired, and sore from working under the house all day. All she wanted was to settle in with a handful of taquitos, a glass of wine, and the latest thriller from Megan Abbott, which she'd just checked out from the local library.

Fuck my life, she thought.

ON MY WAY THERE, she wrote instead.

***

She donned a fresh jumpsuit and thick wool sweatshirt, and with the hood drawn tight, she started across the city on foot. The temperature had dropped in the past hour and her breath steamed as she passed the downtown bars, the town clock, the county jail. She could see little campfires glowing along the San Lorenzo River, silhouettes circling the light. A man was crying somewhere beneath the bridge while another man's voice receded, shouting obscenities across the water. She kept moving, hands stoved in her pockets. A few cars passed under the streetlights, most headed toward the freeway. She moved quickly with her head down. She didn't want anyone to notice her. After another three blocks, she reached the job site, hurried over the rock yard, and climbed the stairs to the front door.

She knocked three times, but no one answered.

The windows were dark, blinds shut. She thumbed at the doorbell, but it looked to have been plastered with house paint many years ago, the button drowned in a thick mauve film.

A quick text to Raoul: NOBODY'S HOME

She waited on the porch for his reply but knew what he was going to say.

JUST CLIMB UNDER AND GET IT, he wrote.

The light from the streetlamps didn't reach far, and the side yard lay hidden in heavy black shadows. She flicked on her phone light and crouched beside the access door, brushing the tall weeds aside. A leggy spider skittered up the wall. Someone had installed a new latch and combination lock since they'd finished the job, but it was all fastened to the same rotten frame. She'd damaged it the last time she'd come through but didn't say anything to Raoul. All it took was a quick yank and the little rotten door popped off the hinges.

She shined her phone light through the small access door and spotted the new pipe section standing toward the back of the crawlspace. It still smelled like sewage and freshly cut iron. She sidled through the door and under the house, panning her phone as she went, hoping the light wouldn't be seen from the outside. It was an awkward dance to hold the phone steady and maneuver among the foundation brackets without using her bandaged hand to steady herself. She'd just spotted the pipe cutter half-buried in a loose patch of dirt when a loud engine motored to the curb out front, mufflers howling and spitting. It sounded like a high-performance sports model.

A car door slammed.

She froze, flicked off the light.

Someone took the front porch steps fast and unlocked the front door. Whoever had entered the house sounded like they were in a hurry. The footsteps raced through the room above her and she heard a loud slap.

Someone toppled to the floor.

"Wake up, you goddamn junkie," said a man with a deep voice. It boomed through the floorboards as if he were standing right on top of her. *"Wake the fuck up."*

A younger man responded with a groggy voice: "What was that for?"

"Where's Zee and Danny Boyd?"

Another pause, followed by another slap.

"Stop it," said the younger voice.

"Two in the house, one on the street. That's the fucking program. *That's always the program.* Now I find nobody on the street and one goddamn junkie on the nod. So where's Zee and Danny Boyd?"

Mirabel didn't know what to do. It was too dark to search for the tool, too dark to move quietly to the door. But she didn't want to risk using her phone light, either. Instead, she made sure the ringer was toggled off and she hunkered down and waited.

"Maybe," said the younger voice, "maybe they're across the street."

"Doing what?"

"There's a bar. Maybe they're just having a quick drink. That's a reasonable thing to do on a Friday night, isn't it?"

"A reasonable thing to do? I'm going to have someone's dick and balls for this. How do you know we didn't get robbed while you were lying there on the nod? What am I gonna see when I open up that trick door? Because let me tell you, it's the difference between life and death. You hear me? *Life and death.*"

"You're gonna see the bag," said the younger man. "That's exactly what you're gonna see. I put it back when the plumbers finished up. Me and Danny Boyd put it right back where it's supposed to go."

"You better hope I see the bag after everything you put me through. Open it."

Movement above. Someone shuffled to the corner of the house and worked a pair of latches loose. A hole appeared above her and illuminated a duffle sitting in the dirt no more than ten feet from where she sat. It wasn't there earlier—she was sure she would have spotted it. She saw a hand reach down through the floor and hoist the bag up through the hole.

"Okay," said the deep voice. "That addresses one concern."

"You want to count it?" said the young man.

"No. I'll count it afterwards."

"After what?"

"After you look through that window and tell me who's parked on the street."

Footsteps—then, *"Oh fuck is that Mr. G?—oh god please no."*

"See the look on Mr. G's face? The way his eyes don't blink? That's the look of a man who just fucking found out."

"Found out what?"

Another slap.

"Don't be obtuse with me."

"Ob—tuse?"

"You know how many buyers got sick off that shit you and Danny Boyd stepped on—*Mr. G's shit*?"

Silence.

"Nothing to say? Enough to make the national news, that's how many. Two dead and twelve in the hospital. What are you doing? Getting on your knees, now? Oh come on. You gonna try to *fellatio* your way out of this?"

"Please. Put the gun away."

"You're not so special, kid. This kind of thing happens all the time. I guarantee a couple of guys like us are doing the same thing in every major city in the world right now. From L.A. to New York to *Kathman-fuckin-du*. One guy with a gun, one guy on his knees. Upon every head a little rain must fall."

A gunshot came, followed by the sound of a body hitting the floor.

Mirabel shuddered. She eyed the access door, but didn't want to risk any noise, not now—not while there was a gun at play. Not if there was someone parked on the street, watching the house. After a few minutes, blood began to seep through the floorboards and she could see it dripping into the dirt beside her, ticking wetly, gathering into a grisly black pond. She heard a zipper open, and a moment later it closed again. The duffle dropped through the hole, then the opening darkened, latches clicking tight.

She heard the man say: *"Goddamn worthless junkie."*

***

The rest of the crew arrived a few minutes later. There was so much yelling and cussing she was afraid there'd be more gunfire. One of them dragged the body into another room and the floor opened up again, the duffle rising—and then lowering—after another raucous altercation. It went on for hours. Sometime after midnight, the arguing fell to silence and the house grew still. Mirabel slipped off her shoe and unpeeled a sock. She lit the flashlight app on her phone and slid it into the sock so it gave the faintest orange glow. Her legs felt numb, and she sat working the blood back into them, crouching against a foundation beam until she could feel her toes. She inched around the puddle of blood as she made her way toward the exit—the last thing she wanted was to leave a trail of bloody footprints out into the street.

The pipe cutter.

She turned back for it—but it was the duffle that caught her eye instead. It sat where they'd left it, the carry straps spooled in the cold dirt. A man was killed over that duffle. It took a crew to keep it safe. And yet those carry straps lay there, waiting for someone to take hold of them, to hoist them over their shoulder and disappear into the night.

She marveled how quiet the house had become—*how still and calm.*

***

"Trace, wake up."

Tracy groaned and palmed the hair from her eyes. She studied the bedroom window, trying to judge the time of day. A thin gray light hung in the blinds—not long after dawn.

"It's early," said Tracy. "I don't have to be at work until—"

"Ever," said Mirabel.

"What?"

"You don't have to go to work ever again."

Tracy watched her with squinted eyes.

"I mean it," said Mirabel. "Come with me. I'll show you."

She'd been up all night stacking and categorizing the contents of the duffle. Best she could tell, it was some kind of go-bag for a high-level drug dealer, with enough valuables to start up a new operation—or cut and run from one in a hurry. Tracy stood in her pajamas with her hands on her hips, the floor crowded with contraband.

"There's seven-hundred thousand dollars in cash," said Mirabel. She tapped three white bricks with her toe. "And look at all that cocaine. From what I just read on my phone, these kilos are worth at least twenty-five grand apiece, depending on the quality. But check this out—" She poured a dozen diamonds from a black velvet bag into her hand. "Fucking diamonds—a bunch of them."

"I don't understand," she said. It was the most engaged she'd looked in months. "Where did you get all this?"

"I stole it," said Mirabel, and her laugh took on a deranged vibe. "From a job site. Here, look at these gold coins. They must be worth another thirty thousand. Gold is crazy expensive right now. You know what this means, Trace? There's over a million dollars lying on our living room floor. We can go anywhere we want. No Vance. No Raoul. No swing shifts at the diner. Just me and you."

Tracy stirred the diamonds around her palm.

"Won't we have to leave town? They'll know you took it, won't they?"

"Sure, they'll figure it out eventually. But we'll be long gone by then." She drew Tracy by the jaw and kissed her hard, sending a couple diamonds clattering onto the hardwood floor. She thought she could feel the sadness draining out of her, that old electricity surging back. "I just bought bus tickets to Portland. The earliest interstate fare I could find. We leave in two hours."

"Two hours?"

"Come on, sad girl. Let's be happy again. It'll be like San Luis, but with the kind of money that won't run out on us. You can write that book you always wanted to—or not work at all. Open a coffee shop if you want. *But we gotta hustle.*"

Tracy's head began a slow bob that reached something resembling agreement.

"You know what?" she said. "Fuck it. I won't miss this place at all. I can't wait to see all the messages on my phone tonight after I blow off work for the last time. Vance is going to have a total meltdown."

"You were always too good for them, Trace," said Mirabel. "Working late, covering every shift they asked you to. Pooling tips with all those losers. They really sucked you dry, those motherfuckers."

***

They were a few miles south of Sacramento when the first text message came through. It was a photo of Raoul with his teeth busted out and blood pouring down his chin. Someone held the tip of a switchblade to his eye and made several deep gashes in the veiny sclera. He wept blood down the crook of his nose like some miraculous Virgin statue. This wasn't a photo of a man stoically facing death—Raoul's face held a certain wild and panicked terror that triggered the hair on the back of Mirabel's neck.

She clicked her phone to black and watched the ranchlands pass along Highway 5, all those muddy cows grazing in the winter grass. Raoul's grisly photo lay on the other side of the little blank screen, just a click away. She felt haunted by it. She wondered if the bag carried a dark curse from which more violence would come. Tracy sat beside her with a book in her lap. She reached across the seat and held her hand.

"Who was that?" she asked.

Mirabel glanced around the bus cabin—half full, mostly college students and elderly. A pasty gray-haired man with a trucker hat gave a dirty look from across the aisle, but she knew it most likely had to do with Tracy holding her hand and not the million dollars in cash and dope hidden in the duffle at her feet.

Mirabel leaned into Tracy and whispered in her ear.

"I think we should change plans," she said. "Maybe buy a car in Sacramento, head east instead. Keep moving for a while. I didn't think this all the way through. Everyone knows we've been wanting to move to Portland—it's where they'll look first."

"You didn't answer me," said Tracy, pointing her chin at the phone. "Who texted you?"

Another message came through. Mirabel was afraid to look—she held the phone in her lap with her fingers laced until the tension broke her. This time they'd sent a screenshot of her last few texts from Raoul, the ones telling her to return to the house on Ocean Street. Another photo came through—a picture of the pipe cutter lying in the dirt beneath the house with the words: FORGET SOMETHING?

"Give me your phone, Trace."

Tracy slid it from her pocket and handed it over. Mirabel coupled their phones together and fed them both through the crack in the bus window where they fell to the highway and skittered under the wheels. They held hands in silence as the ranchlands grew wet and marshy and the city materialized in a thick rind of smog.

***

They ditched the bus and found a shady used car dealership on Stockton Avenue where they traded a kilo of cocaine for an older-model Dodge Charger. Straight-across, no paperwork. The owner, a bearded man with a missing eyetooth and ghostly blue eyes, told them he also owned a salvage yard and it was just as easy to pretend the car got itself cubed. Across the street was a mobile phone shop with a roll-top door and they bought five-hundred dollars' worth of prepaid minutes on a pair of Samsung burners before rolling out of town.

"What if someone reports us missing?" said Tracy. They were ascending the grade through the Sierra foothills, little nests of snow dotting the pine trees on the shadowed side of the high-way. "We'd be all over social media. Then it's just a matter of time."

"Who would report us?"

"My sister. Maybe the girls from the restaurant."

"You haven't spoken to your sister in years."

"I don't know. Maybe she wants to make up all of a sudden."

"We'll find a payphone," said Mirabel. "I still see them out-side convenience stores. Just tell them you're fine and you took a restaurant job in Portland. If someone starts asking questions about us, it'll end right there."

"My god," said Tracy. Her voice sounded sad, but there was also a hint of a smile, a dimple darkening her left cheek. "It feels so reckless. We don't even know where we're fucking going."

"It's safer that way," said Mirabel. "We'll go where the road takes us. If we don't have a plan, how can anyone know where we're going? You having second thoughts?"

"No, just thoughts. That's allowed, isn't it?"

They pulled into Reno just after nightfall. A storm had passed two days before and the city lay buried in a foot of snow. The downtown streets bore the heavy reek of grease traps from the casino hotels. Curds of dirty ice churned in the alleys. On East Fourth they found a motel that took cash by the hour and they lay in bed with the curtains drawn and watched old sitcoms until the city grew calm.

"I'm not gonna sleep tonight," said Tracy later, in the dark. A lone drunk was wandering somewhere out on the street, singing country songs and coughing with a heavy, infected hack. "I'm worried they won't stop looking."

"They're not going to find us," said Mirabel. She was afraid Tracy was losing her nerve, so she said it with as much convic-tion as she could muster. "And every day that passes is closer to when they stop looking for good. This is our chance. The only way to make it in this country is if you're born rich or you get a stroke of wild luck—and everything just came up aces for us.

But you're right—we've got to go farther than one state away, just to be safe. Two or three states away, at least."

"I want to be in a different state in all senses of the word. Does that sound stupid? I want a completely fresh start. Not just for me, but for you too. For both of us. More than anything, that's why I'm still here with you."

The singing man had ebbed into the night, but they could still hear his coughing as if he were the lone survivor of a plague. In the next room, someone flicked on a television and a local newscaster announced herself. Something about a high school football team and more bad weather in the days ahead. They listened for their names.

"That's what you're gonna get, Trace," said Mirabel. "A fresh start. That's what we'll both get. New fucking names and every-thing—I promise you." Then, after a few minutes of silence: "You want to try some of that coke and look at all those dia-monds again?"

***

They took lesser-known highways across the cold Nevada desert. Sun-scoured asphalt and faded yellow lines. Frost glit-tering the sagebrush. They passed reservation towns like Wild Horse and Owyhee, then north to the Snake River along endless miles of feed crops and trundling tractors. They paid cash for everything, and when they couldn't find lodging, they bought heavy wool blankets and slept in the backseat of the Charger.

Raoul's gruesome face haunted Mirabel's dreams.

Those bleeding eyes.

That hollow mouth.

A week later, they'd settled into a single-wide trailer along a lonely stretch of Montana's Route 200. Mostly prairies and oak-studded hills. It was only temporary until they could get everything straightened out—the money, the diamonds, the coke. But most importantly, *the IDs.* There was a methed-out town called Wheat thirty minutes down the road where they'd go for gas and groceries, and even though the town wasn't much, there was some novelty in walking into a grocery store and not checking the prices. Whatever Mirabel wanted went straight into the cart, and she'd buy little things for Tracy on a whim. A blue crystal from a curio shop. A leather coin purse. She found a neighborhood book exchange and she'd bring something new for Tracy to read as soon as she'd finish the last book.

It was a Saturday afternoon in late March—coming back from town with fresh groceries and a new thriller wedged into the dashboard—when Mirabel saw the finger of gray smoke rising from the property. It was their signal. If a stranger were to come down the driveway, the one keeping watch would douse the old Weber kettle with lighter fluid and strike a match. Mirabel raced the Charger down the gravel two-track and left it running as she clambered toward the trailer with an eight-inch hunting knife she kept under the seat.

The trailer had been torn apart. Closet doors ripped from the hinges, cabinets emptied onto the floor. Nobody was inside, but she knew they'd been here. She threw open the wooden drawer under the bed and stared at the empty space where the duffle had been.

"Trace?" she called. No sign of her. No blood, no claw marks on the walls. She wondered if they'd taken her, but that didn't make sense either. She kicked through the boxes of cereal on the floor and ran back outside. She circled the trailer and stood beside the Weber kettle. The flames were still rollicking and heavy smoke pumped over the lot and into the trees beyond. Whatever happened had been recent. *Minutes ago.*

Then she saw her.

A lone figure hovering in the oak trees just a few yards away.

"Oh god, Trace."

They'd hanged her with a bedsheet from a low heavy branch. Still in her pajamas, tangled hair falling all around like tree moss. Mirabel scaled the tree with the knife blade clenched in her teeth like in some old pirate movie and sawed at the bedsheet until Tracy crumpled into the dirt below. She tried to bring her back. She did chest compressions until she heard a rib crack. She felt something caustic and dangerous building inside of her, something made of anger and grief and guilt and fear. It came out in a barbarian scream. A witch's shriek. A sound she'd never heard anyone make before.

Then she remembered the silver car turning west onto HWY 200.

Wasn't it a BMW?

***

She hit a hundred before reaching the highway. By the time the road straightened out past the radio tower, she hit one-forty. Now one-fifty. The world blurred. Only the broken yellow line existed. She didn't care whether she lived or died—she left it all to physics. She passed a tractor that must have been going twenty miles per hour. Then a flatbed pickup. They shrank in the rearview as if they were parked on the highway. After another fifteen minutes a dot appeared on the horizon—maybe three miles away—and every minute that passed, the dot took on more BMW-like traits. Closer still. The weather was turning, and now a light spring rain glossed the roadway.

Her foot stayed planted.

The engine screamed and she screamed alongside it.

The silver car loomed before her.

Closer. Closer.

When she hit the rear bumper, she didn't hit it square. She caught it just under the left rear wheel before a weightless feeling took hold and she felt a cold wind on her skin, a wetness all over. She wasn't sure if she was alive or dead or moving from one state of being to another. She didn't even feel herself hit the ground.

***

Mirabel woke in the prairie grass as two columns of smoke rose over the highway. The rain had intensified. She looked over her wet clothes—some blood, some water. She could only see from her left eye, and when she touched her right eye, it felt full of bloody debris—glass maybe. Or rocks. It took a moment to

45

stand. Not that she felt a lot of pain, but her left arm wouldn't respond—it hung dead and numb like it belonged to someone else entirely. The Charger lay in a smoldering heap by the road shoulder, and on the other side of the highway lay a second heap of twisted metal.

She went limping over the road and approached the car.

Inside, a middle-aged man sat crumpled in the passenger floorboards in a butcher's scrap pile of exposed bones and muscle. She circled the car, peering into every twisted crevice. The trunk had split partly open and she could see the duffle inside. It looked to have survived intact, but there was something else there, too—*Raoul's pipe cutter.* She reached in with her good arm and pulled it out, looked it over. She wondered if they were planning on using it on her as punishment for stealing the duffle. Some kind of sick poetic justice.

Something else caught her eye.

Movement to her right.

Another man was crawling away from the crash on his stomach, leaving a bloody trail in the prairie grass as he went. His clothes had torn mostly off and she could see the dark hairs on his back matted down with rain. She went to him. He'd been crawling with a pistol but looked to have given up and ditched it in the grass. She didn't pick it up. There was a small granite outcropping a few yards away and he was moving toward it inch by inch. Mirabel watched him struggle. The shock was beginning to wear off and now a hard pain grew in her eye cavity and left arm. She thought maybe she'd broken just about every bone on her left side.

"Going somewhere?" she called.

The man stopped moving and tried to look back at her.

Blood was leaking from his ears.

"Fuck off," he said.

She recognized the deep voice from the house on Ocean Street.

She moved closer.

"You didn't have to kill her," said Mirabel. The more she moved her jaw, the worse the pain grew. "I'm the one who took your money. Not her, not Raoul either. All me."

"Leave me alone," he said again.

"Like you left Tracy alone?" She coughed painfully and spat a wad of bloody phlegm in the grass. "I wouldn't have come after you otherwise, you know that don't you? I think you know that."

The man inched forward, heaving and groaning.

"I heard you that day, you know," said Mirabel. "The day I took the bag. You were telling some kid how your situation wasn't unique. How there were always two people somewhere in the world and one person was about to kill the other. *One guy with a gun, one guy on his knees.* Isn't that what you said?"

"It's what I always say," the man said.

"Is that what you told Tracy when you killed her?"

He didn't answer.

"Well, I'm not going to shoot you," said Mirabel. She put a foot on his back, and he stopped trying to crawl. She knelt over him and looped the pipe cutter around his neck like a dog collar. "I'm going to do what you were planning to do to me. I'm going to tighten it until your arteries burst. Now say the rest of the words."

The man could hardly speak.

"What words?" he managed.

"You know the words. The ones you told that junkie before you killed him."

He made a sound that could have been a laugh. Maybe he was choking. She waited. The soil had grown muddy. A flatbed truck had stopped on the highway and there was a man with a cowboy hat pacing on the side of the road with a cell phone to his ear. He gestured at the crumpled BMW, then squinted beyond the wreckage where Mirabel stood hunched and bloody and half-blind like some fearsome fairy tale monster.

"Say it," she said, jerking the pipe cutter, making him bleed. "I want to hear you say it."

Blood gathered around the tiny blades as the man cried out in agony.

"*Upon . . . every . . . head . . . a . . . little . . . rain . . . must—*"

***

It was still raining when the dairy farmer found her sitting at the fenceline, too injured to crawl beneath the barbed wire, too weak to stand. She'd dragged the duffle a half mile from the road and could go no further. A corner of the bag had torn and she'd left a trail of wet cocaine in the prairie grass. The farmer took one look and raised his hat and rubbed his freckled scalp, trying to make sense of what the Good Lord was trying to show him. He cut the fencing with a pair of chanellocks and stood looking at Mirabel with his hands on his hips.

"You dead?" he asked her.

Mirabel didn't say whether she was or wasn't.

When the farmer unzipped the duffle, he whistled and shook his head.

"What kinda trouble you get yourself into, Missy?" He lifted a pair of binoculars from around his neck and glassed the distant highway where he could see all the fire engines and State Troopers and emergency lights blinking through the bad weather. He looked up and down the highway where more Troopers were coming from both directions. "Goddamn," he said. "They're looking for you, aren't they?"

He removed the torn kilo of cocaine and rested it in her blood-stained hands, then hauled the duffle into the barn. He kicked at a pile of loose oat hay until a wood latch appeared in the floor and he squatted over it and pulled it open. A large alloy gun safe lay underneath. He opened it and settled the duffle inside with his arsenal of rifles and ammunition and dirty magazines.

When he returned, he found his wife standing in the rain.

She flicked a finger at Mirabel.

"What the heck's going on, Hubert?" she said. She was shielding her eyes from the rain and shouting over the sound of it hitting the tin-roof barn. "Who's that girl?"

"Reckon she had herself an accident on the highway," he said. "Maybe got confused and wandered out this way."

"Carrying a sack of flour?"

"Pretty sure it's drugs. Left a trail of it straight across the prairie."

"Drugs you say? Oh my word. Is she—*dead*?"

"If she ain't, she'll be getting there quick."

"Ain't that something," she said. "Cousin Ginny's not gonna believe it when I tell her. Shouldn't we call the police?"

"What now?"

"The police."

He looked back across the prairie with the binoculars where he could see one of the Trooper vehicles rolling toward them. He gave a quick glance at the barn again. He was already spending all the money in his head. The high-limit poker tables, steak dinners, fancy cigars. Maybe he'd get himself a red-headed hooker or two. Still, a part of him wondered if the duffle was somehow cursed, that whatever tragedy had befallen the girl would become a mark on his door, too. He'd have to pray on it.

"Looks like they're coming directly," he said. "Bet she's on some kinda wanted list. This is the type of thing that makes the news."

"Ain't that something," she said again. "Cousin Ginny's just not gonna believe a word of this."

No Wrong Way to Grieve

We waited for May at Bull's Cantina, a little wood-paneled dive on the corner of P Street and Nineteenth. Bull's had a decent TV and two-for-one deals on PBR drafts every Thursday afternoon, and it was directly across from the library where we had our weekly meetings. When May finally wandered through the door, she didn't say a word—just held her phone out, eyes fixed on the screen.

"Glad you made it," I said. May liked to sit by the window and watch the traffic on P Street, so I stepped out of the booth and let her slide in. "Tough one today, huh?"

It took her a moment to respond. She glanced at Dante and me and let her eyes drift to the window.

"Tough?" she said. "It was brutal."

Dante rose from the booth and gestured across the bar with one hand on May's shoulder and the other tilting an imaginary drink in the air.

"Can we get both two-for-one pints at once?" he asked.

The bartender looked up and down the bar as if doing a headcount. There were two old men in grease-stained t-shirts watching the TV, a couple sitting in the booth closest to the door. Typical for a weekday afternoon in midtown Sacramento. He uncradled a pair of pint glasses from a stack behind the bar and filled them.

"I'm not supposed to serve both at once," said the bartender as he settled the beers in front of May, foam sliding down the glass onto the lacquered tabletop. "But I don't like being the bad guy, either."

"We know a thing or two about bad guys," I said. "You're practically a saint in our eyes."

We sat in silence and drank. Cars passed on the street, sun filtering low through the oak trees in the park across the way. May was halfway through her first pint when she flipped her phone and showed us her lockscreen photo.

"It's a sunset now," she said. "From the last trip we took together. We wandered out to the cliffs somewhere north of Santa Cruz to watch the sun fade over the water. Ellie spotted a whale so we took a bunch of pictures, but you can't really see it here. She started telling everyone that whales were her new favorite animal."

I set my phone on the table so she could see the lockscreen.

"Changed mine a few weeks ago," I said. "Just after Diaz suggested it. I didn't know what to change it to, so I had my sister do it for me. I think she used the default setting. I like yours, May. I think I have a few sunset pictures if I scroll back far enough. I think it helps. Then again, my life keeps falling apart anyway."

Dante took his phone out, but kept it screen-down on the table. He had a bit of beer foam caught in his mustache and it added to his look of vulnerability.

"You don't have to show us, buddy," I said.

May reached across and held Dante's hand. They sat like that for a moment, eyes getting wet, nothing spoken. He patted May's arm and flipped his phone over. The lockscreen was a Halloween photo of his son, Calvin, in a Spider Man costume. His hair was in braids, and he was missing two front teeth.

"I changed it back," he said. "I missed looking at him every day."

"Diaz says there's no wrong way to grieve," I said.

"Yeah. Just feels like I'm a little behind the group."

"Buddy, we all feel that way sometimes. I know I do."

Another round of drinks came and went. We always joked that our support group required its own follow-up support group, and it wasn't far from the truth. At least the happy hour version came with cheap beer and well drinks, something to numb the raw nerves Diaz exposed.

One of the old men shouted something at the TV and we all looked up.

Usually, it had to do with sports, but this time was different. The bartender had the remote control in his hand, turning up the volume. CNN breaking news. They were zooming over a map of Denfield High School in Arizona as the chyron cycled through the bottom of the screen. The anchor repeated the words GUNMAN and SHOOTING in a maddeningly calm voice.

"I don't fucking believe it," said Dante.

"It's too soon," I said. "Medford happened just a few weeks—"

May pushed me hard, both hands on my shoulder.

"Let me out," she said.

I started to inch out of the booth, but I wasn't fast enough for her. She slapped her hands on the table, hard enough to make the pint glasses rattle on the tabletop. She was telling me to *move my fat ass*. When I climbed out of the booth, she shouldered past me and went straight through the front door and into the daylight. We could see her through the window, dodging the cars on P Street as she fled into the park and disappeared under those big sprawling oak trees.

I locked eyes with Dante.

"Go on," he told me. "I'll settle up here."

***

May lived in a little two-story walk-up in Curtis Park that was just big enough for an adult woman and an overweight tabby cat. Not the best neighborhood, not the worst. I spotted her Ford pickup in the carport, engine ticking as it cooled.

I called Dante from the parking lot, and he picked up on the first ring.

"You find her?" he said.

"Yeah, she drove home. I'm outside her apartment now. Gonna give her a second, then I'll go up and check on her."

"What about you, buddy?"

"Me?"

"Yeah, you," he said. "Don't get in the habit of checking up on everybody without nobody checking up on you."

It's true what they say: when things fall apart, you find out who your real friends are. I'd drifted away from just about every friend I'd had, except Dante. He was the closest thing I had to a best friend.

"I'm alright," I said. "Still in the shock phase, I guess."

"My phone's always on."

I gave it another ten minutes—radio off, phone in the console. Just giving a little space before I knocked. I sent her a quick text before I came up, but she didn't respond. By the time I reached the front door, I could hear her pacing back and forth inside the apartment. When I knocked, the pacing stopped.

"May, it's me."

A long pause, then: "It's not a good time."

She sounded angry, voice cracking.

"I know it's not a good time," I said. "It's a really bad fucking time. That's why I'm here. I want to see you, make sure you're okay."

"Well, I'm not okay."

I knocked again, louder this time.

"May, please. Open up, pal."

The deadbolt clicked and the doorknob rattled.

I opened the door and found her leaning against the wall with her arms folded. At her feet stood a half-full bottle of generic vodka. She'd been crying, and her tears had made muddy mascara trails down her cheeks. Cobwebs stirred in the corners of the room when I entered, and beneath the windowsill sat a trio of withering houseplants, leaves scattered on the hardwood floor. It was just another American home where not long ago, a bookish young girl never returned from school—and in that way it wasn't any different than mine.

When I hugged her, my eyes drifted to the dining table where she'd printed out a pile of maps and spread them over the table-top.

But that wasn't all.

On the chair hung a few yards of rope and a pair of bolt cutters. I spotted an acetylene torch, a large crowbar—all brand new. I went to the table and picked up an oddly shaped tool that looked like some kind of fancy bottle opener and gave it a close inspection.

"What the hell is this thing?" I asked.

She took a drink and stood watching me for a moment.

"It's a universal tank wrench, Luís."

"Oh. I bet I can open a beer with it."

"There's beer in the fridge. Give it a shot."

It turned out the universal tank wrench made an excellent beer opener. I sat on the couch, took a few sips of the microbrew she'd been stocking up on, not saying anything at first. I wanted to ask about the odd assortment of tools, but I didn't know how to start.

"It's this thing I've been doing," she said, gesturing at the table. "Whenever there's a new shooting, I add a piece to it. By now, I have almost everything I need."

I sifted through the maps. From what I could tell, it all centered around a large building at the edge of the Nevada desert.

"You gonna break into Area 51?"

"No." She offered a barely-there laugh. "Why would I do that?"

"Then what's all this?"

"It's where they make them, Luís."

I studied the map again as if her clue would change things. Still, I was lost.

"Where *who makes what*?"

"It's where they make the AR-15s that killed our kids."

***

She said it was therapy.

Just something to feel a bit of empowerment amid the crushing powerlessness of the U.S. gun control movement. I could sympathize with her revenge fantasy, even though it was something I couldn't actually get behind. We'd all gone to the protests, participated in the boycotts, written to the politicians. We'd donated what we could afford to the right causes. But the shootings kept coming, and with few exceptions, they all involved the same weapon—or some variation of it.

"So, I started to plan," she said. "A little bit here and there. Just something to stay sane, to see if it could even be done." She was still working on the bottle, and I wasn't going to stop her. May was a sleepy drunk, the kind who nodded off without much of a fuss—and I could tell she was getting close.

"But then something crazy happened," she said.

"What happened?"

"Something totally unexpected."

"Tell me."

"I came up with a really good fucking plan."

It had me very concerned, but she was talking, that was the main thing. The booze kept her forthcoming, which under the circumstances was better than the quiet, guarded version of May that typically showed up. In fact, she wouldn't stop talking about that big factory at the edge of the desert and her menagerie of strange items.

But something began to percolate—something that fluttered softly at the back of my skull like moth wings. I couldn't nail it down at first, nor did I really care to. But soon the fluttering grew into a deep and unbearable agitation, a great tortuous itch. It wasn't until after I'd put May to bed and locked the door up tight and was cruising under the dim orange streetlights back to Bull's Cantina that I finally realized what was eating me up so bad:

It really was a good fucking plan.

***

It took time for Dante to come around.

But I could tell the moment it started fluttering at the back of his skull, too—when it shifted from an abstract idea to a thing of potential. And soon we were all talking about it together. May's apartment became the new Bull's. We'd drink and look over the map and test the acetylene torch. We'd role-play all the other bits and pieces of the plan until we'd made the whole scheme that much more likely to succeed. We kept telling ourselves that's all it was—some kind of experimental role-play therapy. And it was effective. You could *feel* the catharsis. I don't know how many times we met up to talk about it—eight, maybe ten times. But sometime after the next shooting, after the next gut-wrenching, soul-crushing, maddening time—this one at a middle school in South Carolina—we found ourselves driving east through the Sierra Nevadas in a cold-plated pickup with the sun setting behind us, heading toward a factory on the edge of the Nevada desert.

***

It was just before midnight when we cut the chain guarding access to an abandoned copper mine and wheeled through the complex. There wasn't much left but a few outbuildings and toppled utility lines, sagebrush growing up through the scrap piles of industrial debris. I killed the headlights and parked along the western perimeter, looking out over the open desert. We gathered there in the scrub, taking turns with the binoculars. About a half mile to the southwest we could see the industrial park, just a collection of anonymous gray buildings glowing yellow under an array of security lights. Nothing between here and there but flat, dry, desert.

"Far as I can tell, nothing's changed," said May. She clicked a little LED pen light and looked over a freshly printed cache of Google satellite images. "I've been staring at these photos for months now, and everything looks the same. Like they were all taken yesterday."

Dante lowered the binoculars, gave a quick nod.

"It's just like we planned," he agreed. "The tank, the rolltop door. But no security detail yet. I'll feel a lot better once I see them do a leg or two. Ready to get a closer look?" He slipped on a ski mask and situated the eyeholes just right. You can rehearse a plan till you know it front to back, but when the ski masks go on, let me tell you—those adrenaline glands start squirting the good shit.

The hardest part was carrying the floor dollies. Dante and I each had one strapped to our backs, the straps repurposed from old thrift store backpacks. May wore a pack of her own, fashioned to carry the acetylene tank and related gear. The rest of it was light: ropes, zip ties, small tools.

We'd walked ten minutes across the dark of the desert when Dante raised his binoculars and signaled for us to stop.

"There he is," he said, glassing the complex. "Little white truck, cruisin' slow."

We could see it with our naked eyes. The truck reached the end of the building and parked for a moment, headlights on. Then the driver got out, walked to the edge of the property and stood, taking a piss. When he finished, he climbed back into the truck, waited a minute or two, and drove back the other direction.

"We've been here thirty minutes and that's the first we've seen security," I said. I watched the truck as it headed toward the main road and disappeared behind a storage rental company. "We have at least that much time starting now. Do we go?"

I thought maybe we'd each give a final confirmation, or offer some last-minute chance to back out and say *at least we made it this far*. But May marched forward without a word, and Dante quickly followed. I watched as they headed toward that gray building haunted by sickly yellow lights—haunted by much more than that, really—then I worked up the nerve and followed the rest of the way.

***

We stepped off the scrub and came up on the rear of the building. No signage, no fencing. No trucks parked along the road with logos or insignias—nothing to suggest what they manufactured inside. A single rolltop door stood along the back wall near a large dumpster, and about twenty yards from the door sat a pill-shaped, five-hundred-gallon propane tank, about ten feet long and three feet wide. Dante and I began working the tank onto the dollies one end at a time, while May crouched beside the rolltop with the torch in her hand. We kept silent, and so far, everything was exactly how we'd planned—except that the tank was heavier than I thought it would be. A quick look under the valve lid showed it was at seventy-five percent capacity. Still, between the two of us, it didn't take long to get the whole thing rolling. When we were done with the tank, we wheeled the dumpster out from the side of the building. It was heavy, too. Almost overflowing. May had determined that garbage day was tomorrow, and that became another element in her plan. We found a few wood pallets leaning against the building and threw those on top for good measure.

May was finishing up, bright sparks casting over her shoulder, the strange, garlicky smell of acetylene and hot steel filling the air. She'd cut a three-foot rectangle in the rolltop but hadn't yet removed it from the door.

"Once I kick it in, we've got to hustle," she whispered. "In and out."

I glanced at the road, back across the dark of the desert.

Everything was so calm and quiet.

Just the low, soft hum of transformers atop the utility poles.

"I'm ready," I said, and looked at Dante.

I could see his eyes tinseled in the dim glow of the security lights.

"I'm so fuckin' ready for this," he said, wiping the tears with his sleeve. "We should have done this years ago. I fuckin' love you guys."

We hugged him, and now my eyes were wet too.

"We're in this together, buddy."

May squared off with the door and kicked the rectangle out of the rolltop and crawled through. A high-pitched alarm erupted from somewhere in the building. No going back, now—all or nothing. She unlatched the door from the inside and rolled it up into the guide and Dante and I began wheeling the propane tank through. We were inside the loading bay, stacks of AR-style rifles boxed and shrink-wrapped onto wood pallets. Which of those rifles would cause another breaking news event was anyone's guess. At the far end of the bay was a large door that led to the main shop floor. We pushed the tank so it was right up against the door, and I flipped open the valve lid and began working the handwheel to the main valve. I unhooked the bolt cutters from my belt and held them up in the air—just to signal what I was about to do—and then I bore down and cut the pigtail line between the main valve and the regulator. A cold, malevolent hiss filled the loading bay along with the raw, eggy smell of propane.

I hurried back outside and found May by the dumpster, relighting the acetylene torch.

Her eyes met ours.

Dante and I both gave a nod.

She tossed the lit torch into the dumpster, and we pushed the whole thing through the bay door and let it coast as far as it could under its own momentum. We could already see the pallets beginning to light. Soon the whole thing would catch, trash and all. I always felt a dumpster fire was an appropriate metaphor for American gun culture—but tonight it was literal.

We pulled the rolltop down and let it cook.

"That's it," said May. She had her hands slightly up, fingers splayed as if she'd just placed the winning piece on a board game. "That's everything. The whole plan."

"There's still the part about not getting caught," I said. "Come on, let's go."

When we turned to leave, a thin young man in a black and yellow reflective jacket and polyester uniform appeared on the road with a flashlight in his hand. He had a thin, soft-looking mustache like kids try to grow in junior high. A handheld radio clicked and screeched from his hip. Behind him sat the white pickup truck, headlights shining crookedly, a shiny security emblem fixed on the side. The loading bay was beginning to flicker through the hole we'd cut, shadows twisting all around us.

He saw our masked faces and backpedaled, raised the radio to his face.

We'd discussed what would happen if security found us. None of us wanted to bring weapons, so the idea was to rush together and overwhelm them with sheer body mass.

Dante reached him first, sent him reeling backward onto the road. The radio went skittering over the asphalt and then Dante was on top of him, fists swinging down. The security guard put up a fight, but it didn't last long. When Dante stood again, the young man's nose was bloody, and he looked asleep.

"We can't leave him here," said Dante. "He's too close to the building."

"So are we," I said, nervously.

The light coming from the loading bay was very bright now. I imagined the dumpster completely engulfed, pallets searing and blackening like matchsticks, flames eager for the taste of a few hundred gallons of propane.

"Fuck it," said Dante. "He's coming with us."

He sat the security guard up and folded him over his shoulder and we hurried into the scrub, none of us looking back until we were at least a hundred yards out. We stopped and Dante set the security guard down, breathing hard. The man was beginning to wake, groaning and trying to push himself up. We all stood watching the factory as the smoke grew thicker and thicker. The night sat black and starry over the desert and the smoke just disappeared into all that darkness at first. But when the first explosion came, the whole scene changed. The ground shuddered. Fire corkscrewed through the heavy black smoke and carried off in the beautiful twisting weather it created.

I imagined all the deadly things inside now warping, glowing red.

"I know what this is about," said the security guard. His nose bled heavily, gathering in a gory mess along the neck of his undershirt. He didn't seem scared or angry at all. He sat with his hands on his knees, watching the building burn. "It's about that school shooting, isn't it? In South Carolina? They told us something like this could happen."

"No," I said. "It's not about South Carolina." May gave me a flat angry look through the holes of her mask. I wasn't supposed to talk to anyone if I didn't need to. That was one of the rules she'd strictly laid out. "It's about all the shootings before that, too."

The young man nodded in the dark.

"Well, you guys are doing something about it, I'll give you that." He wiped his nose and looked at the mess on the back of his hand. "Nobody else is doing a goddamn thing. Want to know something? I don't know why I'm telling you this, but I got a little nephew—my sister's kid. Sweetest kid you'd ever meet. Smart, too. You know the first thing I thought when he started kindergarten? *I hope to God he isn't shot on the first day of school.* I couldn't shake it. I guess I'm not the only one who worries about it, huh?"

Another explosion. This one bigger and more colorful than the last. A searing, red-orange flower rose over the desert. I took a step back when the sound hit us. When it receded, I could hear sirens coming from somewhere in the far distance. One thing we wondered about was how much ammunition they kept on site for testing—all that red hot shrapnel flying every direction at twice the speed of sound. Maybe the fire department wouldn't risk getting close. They'd probably stage on the highway and let it burn, mop up the ashes afterwards.

I unhooked the pack of zip ties from my belt and showed it to May, but she waved me off. Instead, she pulled a fresh ski mask from her bag and slipped it backwards over the security guard's head like a blindfold.

"Don't pay attention to which direction we go," she said.

"I didn't see a thing," said the young man.

***

We kept to our schedules the best we could.

Our nine-to-five jobs, the Thursday afternoon support group.

We drank two-for-one beers at Bull's, and hard as it was, we didn't mention that night in the Nevada desert.

Three weeks passed, and we were a couple rounds deep when the bartender came around with the TV remote, clicking up the volume. We exchanged glances, took each other's hands. That sinking, rotten, gut-punch of a phrase BREAKING NEWS flashing across the screen.

"Crazy," said the bartender. "That's the third time this month."

On the screen was aerial footage of a beige building in some Arkansas industrial park. Black smoke billowing from the windows. The chyron declared that another firearms manufacturer had caught fire under suspicious circumstances. The FBI and the ATF were about to give a joint press conference, but there were no suspects.

It was certainly news to us.

"If you're looking to buy an assault weapon, it's already too late," said the bartender. He'd wandered over to our booth with his bald head sadly shaking, showing us a listing for an AR-style rifle on his phone. "Look. They're going for a few grand or more on account of all this nonsense. I saw one going for six-thousand dollars just now. Can you believe it? I paid six hundred for mine a couple years ago. Just ain't American if you ask me. This whole business is gonna start a civil war, I bet you."

"I say bring it on," said May. "Maybe we'll be too busy killing one another to bother with the school kids for a while. I'll trade you one civil war for a dozen classrooms full of living children any day." She laughed, sort of a wild and ominous laugh. I wouldn't say she looked happy—far from it. None of us really looked happy anymore. But at the very least, we all felt the world had tilted a degree or two on its axis because of what we'd done, and if it kept on tilting, maybe that wouldn't be so bad.

We watched the news and drank, and the night slipped away from us. We showed each other our new lockscreen photos. Pictures of our kids with big gap-toothed smiles. We shared other photos and videos too. Birthdays. Easter egg hunts. Halloween nights with pillowcases full of candy. We decided Diaz was mostly full of shit, that the whole world should be a monument to our beautiful kids. But we also conceded he was right about one thing—maybe there really was no wrong way to grieve.

We stayed until the bar closed and then we stumbled into the city lights and went arm in arm into the park where those humongous oak trees reached over the grass. May suddenly stopped and opened one side of her coat. She'd somehow stashed a half-full pint of beer there, and she raised it up in a sloppy toast, foam getting all over her hands, all over us, too. She glanced around the park to make sure we were alone.

"Here's to a good fucking plan," she said, drinking.

Dante took the glass and drank, then handed it to me.

I glanced around, too. Just be sure.

"No," I said. "Here's to a great one."

The Hour is Getting Late

Delmore stood on the riverbank under a cheap drug store umbrella, watching a windless downpour fall over the Cumberland. He'd just let a call from his brother's wife go unanswered, hoping she'd text instead. Now she was calling a second time, and he knew if she called twice already, there'd be a third. When he finally picked up, she didn't wait for him to say hello.

"Where are you, Buddy?" She said it with heat, like she'd been expecting him all night. "I cooked for you, dammit."

"Downtown," he said. "Watching the river."

"That all?"

"Watching the river and thinking about Beau."

She went silent, an old Bob Dylan song playing in the background. He could hear the glass door unlatch and slide open. The zip of a cigarette lighter. The music cut out and now all he heard through the tiny speaker was bad weather.

"Want to guess what I'm doing?" she said.

"Maybe you're watching the river and thinking about Beau, too."

"Well ain't you some kinda clairvoyant."

"Didn't figure you were gonna cook, Joelle. I woulda been there."

"It was gonna be a surprise. I could heat it up, you know—if you're hungry."

A flock of geese called out in the dark, somewhere on the far bank. It wasn't long after nightfall, and the Shelby Street Bridge was full of lone figures coming and going. The Nashville skyline pulsed and flowed, little squares of light blinking down the high-rise facades.

"Got any booze in the house?" he asked.

"Not a drop. I was trying to support your brother. Somebody had to."

"Mind if I bring enough for the two of us?"

She took another drag and let it out slow.

"Well. I don't suppose it matters much anymore."

***

He pulled into the driveway an hour later and parked beside his brother's powder-blue GMC pickup with the 70s-era camper on top. He patted the camper shell and twisted the aluminum doorknob. How many nights had he slept here after a show? Too many to remember. A hundred sounded right. He peeked into the dark of the camper—the single-burner stove, the brown

70

cabover bed. Cigarette burns leering from the carpet. He could live his whole life and never smell that combination of odors again—sweat, liquor, a hint of diesel. Beau had spilled a bong once, and maybe that was the x-factor, the thing that made the smell so singular.

"Dinner's getting cold for the second time." Joelle was coming up the walkway in her wool boots and pajamas, curly blond hair pulled back. The rain had let up and there was a wet coolness coming up off the front lawn. She gestured at the old camper. "Make me heat it up again and that's where you're sleeping tonight. Lord knows Beau spent plenty a night in that ol' thing."

"Hey, Joelle." he said, and hugged her.

"Hey yourself, stranger."

She led him into the dusky brick house where he could smell the richness of a home cooked meal and the stale funk of tobacco smoke. Family photos on the walls, yellowed and slightly off-kilter. A roster of the dead and distant. She went to the kitchen and brought out a plate with a heaping scoop of shepherd's pie, a side of greens, and a buttered biscuit. She came back again with two empty glasses and set them on the table. Delmore slipped a fresh bottle of whiskey from his jacket pocket, uncorked it, and poured generously.

They touched their glasses together and invoked Beau's name.

"That was nice, what you said at the funeral," said Joelle.

"I wrote it months ago," he said. "I knew things were getting rough, but I never thought it would end quite like this."

"How long you planning to stay?" The way she said it was like she was trying not to sound interested, but was. "The room's made up. Baby's sleeping with me."

"A couple nights if it's all right. Ran into C-Bone at the funeral. You probably saw us talking. Man, he hasn't changed a bit. Wants me to play a set at The Blue. You know, kind of a tribute to Beau."

Joelle sat straight in her chair, studying him.

"You're playing tonight, ain't you?"

Delmore drank what was left in the glass. "Yes ma'am."

"At the same damn club your brother was killed two weeks ago?"

"That's about the long and short of it."

"You ain't gonna play that song are you?"

"Well."

"When I married into this family, I knew most of you were stupid, but not the whole damn lot."

"You figured I was the smart one?"

"No. I figured you were the least stupid one."

When Delmore finished his meal, he carried the dishes back to the sink and cleaned them and set them out on the drying rack. When he returned, Joelle was sidling into the room with a guitar case in her hand. She laid it atop the kitchen table with the latches facing Delmore as if it were part of some unspoken ceremony.

"Before you open it, you oughta know I ain't washed the blood off yet."

Delmore spread his hands over the rough tweed case. He looked at Joelle and she gave a rueful smile and touched his shoulder. He'd seen his brother's body in the oakwood casket, spent and cold. A specter face that twinned his own. Those once-lightning fingers now folded and still.

But this.

This brown tweed case with silver latches and a mother-of-pearl handle.

This was where his spirit lay.

***

The club looked busy when he arrived, with a line spilling onto the sidewalk that stretched halfway down the block. Delmore didn't figure they'd come to see him. His name wasn't even on the marquee. But a few in the crowd recognized him and came up to give their condolences. He nodded to the bouncer—a pair of biceps with a head named Moustapha—who slapped a meaty hand on Delmore's shoulder and guided him through the rope line.

"Got your back, Buddy," said Moustapha. "Already found two ankle pieces and a pig sticker. Ain't nothing getting through tonight. I'm the motherfuckin' TSA."

"Well, I ain't played in over a month," said Delmore. "I'm worried about them beer bottles coming my way more'n anything else."

"Shit. You never played a bad song in your life."

"You checkin' tattoos?"

"88s, SS bolts, swastikas—you bet."

"Good. Where's C-Bone?"

Moustapha pointed his chin toward the bar.

"You know where C-Bone is."

Delmore wended through the back tables with the guitar case at his side, past silhouetted couples with cocktails pillared between them, hands searching each other's laps. Blue neon sizzling up the walls. A solo pianist was banging out a twelve-bar boogie on the spotlit stage, doing his best Little Richard impression. He even had the makeup and the little pencil-thin mustache. Some musicians looked down on the cover acts, but not Delmore. Butchering a song you wrote was one thing—most times nobody knew the difference. Make a mistake on an old standard and that's when the glass starts to fly.

At the end of the bar sat a middle-aged Black man with a short gray beard, an old leather-bound account ledger opened before him and a bottle of Jameson at arm's reach. He eyed Delmore in the bar mirror and reached across for a clean glass and poured what was left of the bottle.

"Goddamn, it's Buddy Delmore," said C-Bone. They slapped palms together like they'd done it a thousand times. Maybe they had. "In all this neon light, I almost thought you were your brother's ghost. Almost."

Delmore lifted his case. "With his old guitar, I don't blame you."

"Oh damn," said C-Bone. He handed Delmore the whiskey glass and gently took the case. "What a treat. Mind if I lay this baby out on the bar? I wanna take a look at her."

"Just so you know, it ain't been cleaned yet."

C-Bone toweled the bar with a terry cloth rag and carefully set the case onto the lacquered mahogany as if he were laying a baby in a bassinet. He flicked the clasps and gently lifted the case lid. Delmore thought he was holding his breath—maybe they both were. Inside, lay Beau Delmore's Gibson J45, nestled in a bed of blue velveteen. A grisly, blackish stain marred the tobacco finish, down across the pearl inlays and over the bridge. Some of it gathered on the strings like shop grease. C-Bone reached for the terry cloth rag, but Delmore caught him by the wrist.

"Leave it," said Delmore.

C-Bone dropped the rag. "Sorry, brother."

"I want everyone to see. It's the reason I agreed to do this."

"I feel you, baby. So, you gonna play the song?"

"I don't know what the hell I'm gonna play."

C-Bone reached into his pocket and looked at his phone. He swiped and tapped out a message and slipped it back into his pocket. Whatever he'd read on the screen drained all the playfulness out of him.

"Listen, Buddy," he said. "Me and the guys want to show you something after your set. It's a little bit of a drive, maybe thirty minutes. So come find me after, okay? It's important."

"If it's about my brother, I want to know now."

C-Bone glanced around the club, chewing his lip.

He leaned in close.

"Can't say nothing now. But you gotta come. You just gotta, that's all. We done better than the cops, is all I'm saying. We shook every damn tree in the great state of Tennessee till something rotten dropped out. That's about all I can say about it right now."

The stage lights brightened. The pianist jumped onto the piano bench, blew the crowd a kiss, and took a sweeping bow. Applause filtered through the room as the house music came on—some old Lightnin' Hopkins tune from the 1950s.

"I'll come find you," said Delmore.

C-Bone gave a knowing grin and closed the guitar case.

"Hell yeah, you will. Have a great set, Buddy."

***

Delmore hunkered onto the stool with one boot on the foot rung and the other flat against the stage. The house lights dimmed. He waited as the hollers and whistling subsided, till everyone got a good look at the bloodstained guitar on his knee. Someone shouted *we love you, Buddy*—and others quickly joined in. When the room fell silent again, he fretted a minor chord and strummed. It wasn't a song he knew, or a song anyone had ever heard. He let the guitar tell him what to play. He raked a sad little riff up on the fifth fret and went back into the chord again. He kept playing. After a few minutes, his fingers found the chords Beau had played when his killer gunned him down. *A Minor, C Major, D Minor Seven*. All open position—more intimate, honest. He played the way his brother played—a deep, resonant strum from top to bottom, straight down the sound-hole for maximum volume. The rhythm was a slow, hypnotic lullaby. And when he sang, it was with Beau's cadence. *Beau's words.* He sang the lines exactly as his brother wrote them, about the wickedness of men and the damage they deal. The poisonous cycles of violence. He sang about the very worst men in town, and he called them out by their names—just as his brother had done.

Let me tell you 'bout Robert Klein
He shot Billy G at Twelfth and Pine
Let me tell you 'bout that man Klein
He'll be dead before his time

***

After his set, Delmore took HWY 24 south toward Murfreesboro, following C-Bone's Lincoln Continental past acres of industrial warehouses and barren elm tree groves. He didn't want to ride with C-Bone if he didn't have to—better to ride solo so he could leave quickly if he didn't like whatever he had to show him. Thirty minutes passed and the Lincoln eased off the highway toward a seedy strip of cheap motels and fast-food joints. Delmore followed close behind. A sickly yellow sign glowed in the parking lot that read BIG ANU'S MOTEL. It looked like they'd once advertised a color TV, but that quadrant of the sign had been concealed by a reckless slather of mauve paint.

He parked and stepped out into the dirt lot, looking up at the highway at all the big rigs barreling through the night toward Chattanooga and beyond. C-Bone was walking over with a lit cigarette clenched in his teeth and his hands stoved in the pockets of his wool coat.

"Goddamn," said Delmore, gesturing at the sign. "What's going on at the Big Anus Motel?"

"The apostrophe is important," said C-Bone, with a laugh. "Anu Biggs is a friend. And any friend of mine is a friend of yours. When we need to keep a low profile outside the city, she's happy to help—no questions asked."

"That's what we're doing here? Keeping a low profile?"

"Yes sir." He nodded to a ground-level room at the end of the row. The whole place felt invisible from the highway, like they'd taken the offramp and pulled a blackout curtain down behind them. "Come on, Buddy, he's waiting."

"Who's waiting?"

"Just come with me."

He followed to room 118. C-Bone paused at the door and hammered out a quick text and waited. A few seconds later, the security latch unclasped and the door opened. There were two men he knew standing just inside the room—musicians from around Nashville. One they called Jimmy Fingers, and the other was a one-armed trumpeter called Hot Dog. They greeted Delmore with knowing eyes and turned to let him enter. On the floor, by the foot of the bed, lay a gagged and bloodied man restrained with zip ties and nylon cording.

"This here's Devil," said C-Bone. He knelt over the man and hoisted him to his knees by his sweaty blond hair. On his chest was a fresh black swastika tattoo. 88s on both forearms. He looked like a dictionary of Nazi iconography. "He's the one who killed Beau. Thought you might want to tell him what you think of him before we take turns beating him to death."

"That true, Devil?" said Delmore. "You kill my brother?"

The bound man rolled a bloodshot eye at Delmore and mumbled through his gag. He bunched his face, snorting and scowling. He seemed to be nodding in the affirmative to Delmore's question and daring everyone to kill him right there on the spot.

"You killed Beau 'cause he sang about your dumb Nazi club?" said Delmore. "Don't seem like an appropriate response to a man's artistic expression. But I don't suppose fascists care about such liberties." He motioned to Jimmy Fingers, who passed a bottle of whiskey from the bedside table. Delmore drank deeply and handed it back. "Or was it because our daddy was Black? See, that's the thing I don't understand about you neo-Nazi types. You honestly believe if you somehow bent the world to your political viewpoint, your life would improve? Like they'd give you a nice bank job and marry you off to some beautiful high-class woman with a pedigree and a kindly manner? You think the new fascist regime would trip all over themselves to name a boulevard after you? Give you some kind of robe and an honorary title? Because I guarantee if your shit-for-brains political fantasies ever came true, you'd still be a corner boy with no job and a gram-a-day meth habit. Just a lonely old turd circling the drain, same as now. Nothing would change for you. Absolutely fuck-all." He pulled the rag from Devil's mouth and with it came a drizzle of bloody foam. "You got something to say about all this, fella?"

"When my brother finds you," said Devil, rocking his shoulders back and forth against the restraints, "he gonna gut you like a Ju-ly trout. You gonna wish you ain't never been born."

"Me and him got more in common than I figured," said Delmore. "We both try to look after our brothers."

"Then he gonna come after your whole family. *Women and children first.*"

Delmore stuffed the rag back into Devil's mouth.

"Figured you were gonna say something like that next."

Hot Dog flipped a small aluminum bat in the air and caught it on the fat end with the handle extended toward Delmore.

"You want the first whack, brother?"

Delmore took the bat, looked it over thoughtfully.

"I appreciate all this, fellas," he said. "But I don't believe I got it in me. Beau wouldn't't've liked it much either, to tell the truth. The Delmore Brothers always tried to strike an optimistic tone about the world. All the same, I know Devil ain't leaving this motel room alive, so you fellas just go ahead and do what needs to be done. Don't seem like this could end but one way."

C-Bone put a hand on Delmore's shoulder. "I figured this might be outside your comfort zone, but I wanted you here nonetheless. Give your family a sense of closure. The brother he's talking about is Robert Klein. The name should sound familiar to you."

"One of the names in Beau's song."

"That's right. Don't worry, Buddy—this whole thing's coming to a close, now. Just wait outside and I'll let you know when it's done—unless you want to come in at the end? I understand either way."

"No, I'd rather you tough guys handle it. Besides, ol' Jimmy Fingers is starting to get that itchy look in his eyes."

"Sure thing, Buddy."

Delmore went to the car and lifted Beau's guitar from the case. In the dark, the bloodstains looked like black lacquer. He sat on the hood with his boot heels propped on the chrome bumper and played his brother's favorite songs while those big engines roared down the highway and the percussive sounds of a dying devil rang out from the sleazy motel room.

***

It was long past midnight when he returned to Joelle's house. The neighborhood was dark, streetlights faintly glowing through the river mist. He'd parked in the gravel driveway and was pulling the guitar case out of the trunk when he heard the baby crying. He checked his phone. 2:45am. The walkway was slick with leaves and he stepped carefully toward the front door. He reached for the doorknob and paused. A fresh crack ran up the jamb, yellowish wood underneath.

The baby's squall wouldn't quit.

"Joelle?"

He nudged the door open with the end of the case.

In the living room stood a tall man with receding blond hair pulled into a braided ponytail. He had the same '88' tattoos on his forearms as Devil. Webs on his elbows, SS bolts on his neck. In the crook of his arm lay the baby, wheeling her tiny hands in the air, crying for her mother.

Then he saw Joelle lying face-down in the kitchen.

A bloody handprint on the wall.

"Why don't you set the baby down," said Delmore. He made his voice low and monotone like someone might talk to a spooked horse. "We can talk about whatever this is outside."

"I don't think so," said the man, tickling the baby's chin. "I think she likes me."

Delmore looked him up and down. Stained jeans, leather boots. He wore a sleeveless t-shirt with a rip in the gut like he'd narrowly escaped a knifing. Blond stomach hair poking through.

"You one of Devil's buddies?"

The man's eyes sparked with interest.

"Now how'd you guess a thing like that?" He was rocking the baby, but it wasn't soothing her. The cries only grew angrier. "Been looking all over town for him. Figured you showing up and my brother going missing was too much of a coincidence."

"You Robert Klein?"

The man took an insincere bow.

"Give her over and I'll tell you where Devil is," said Delmore.

"That deal don't work for me." There was a loud sputter from the kitchen. Both men looked. Joelle's leg twitched and she sputtered again, struggling for air. "Bring my brother, then you get the baby. Maybe there'll be time to save the baby's mama if you're quick about it, but I doubt it, given the way her face hit the counter."

"Well, I guess we're both in luck," said Delmore.

"How's that?"

"You're brother's already here, fella."

Klein stopped rocking the baby and darted his cold gray eyes around the room.

"Bullshit."

"His head is, anyway. Right here in my guitar case, tied off in a trash bag. I got tired of hearing all that Nazi shit and I did him biblically." Delmore slid his index finger across his throat. "That shut him up real fuckin' quick."

Klein slipped a big silver revolver from behind his back and pointed it one-handedly at Delmore.

"You're lyin'. Open it."

"See for yourself."

Delmore set the case on the coffee table and unclasped the latches. He'd only have one shot at this, and he doubted it would work. Still, there wasn't much else he could do to save the baby—and whatever might be left of Joelle. He took the guitar by the neck and lifted it out and began to search the empty case as if there were some secret compartment that could harbor an entire human head.

"I know I put it in here," said Delmore. "Just give me a second."

Klein looked like he was about to comment when Delmore swung the guitar like a fat paddle. The gun flew, clattered against the wall. The baby toppled and rolled screaming onto the shag carpet. Delmore reached for her, but Klein moved on him. He jabbed again with the guitar and caught the man under his jaw. It sent him back a step. They stood at a stalemate for a second or two—the baby screaming all the while—but Delmore knew he'd done well. Klein had given up the baby and the gun, and now Delmore was the only one with a weapon of sorts. He had a chance.

Another swing—but this time the man took hold of the guitar and wrested it out of Delmore's hands. He choked up on the neck and bashed it against the brick fireplace and threw the splintered thing with its slack strings clattering across the room.

"Bad move, Buddy," he said, wiping blood out of his mouth. "You dumb sonofabitch. I might've let the baby live."

Then he dove for the gun.

Delmore jumped on top of him. They grappled. It devolved into a slow-moving wrestling match with the barrel of the gun inching closer and closer to Delmore's forehead. They rolled a half-turn so now Klein was mostly on top, grinning and drooling, SS lightning bolts standing taut on his greasy neck.

Delmore thought he was a dead man.

Except—*the baby stopped crying.*

The jarring absence of sound made the two men look up.

Joelle came hobbling toward them like some graveyard ghoul with the baby clutched tightly to her chest, a ten-inch kitchen knife dangling in the other hand. Her nose was split at the bridge and her front teeth were bloody slots. She muttered something that could've been a *fuck you,* then she reared up and fed the knife to Robert Klein's pale white neck.

***

They were halfway to Saint Thomas Hospital under a gloomy morning sky. The way those black clouds loomed over the city, Delmore wondered if the sun would ever come out again. He could hear the baby nursing in the back seat, Joelle humming some old lullaby. Without thinking, he joined in, his tune merging with hers, until he realized he was humming the same song he'd sung earlier that night. The song that named Klein.

Other than Beau's song, Delmore had heard the man's name over the years whispered in the sleaziest dives on South Broad. Now Klein and his brother Devil were just a couple of back-alley boogeymen who'd haunted their last street corner. Delmore had used the revolver to finish the man—although, the way Joelle made him choke on that knife, the bullet felt like an undeserved act of mercy.

He caught her watching him in the rearview.

"You fought for us, Buddy," she said, the words slurring through her vacant teeth. She'd passed out twice already from the concussion, so he was happy to hear her voice. "Both of us know why, we just ain't said it yet."

"I would have fought for you no matter what. You're family."

"Don't play dumb. You know what I'm talking about."

Delmore looked back to the road. The rain had picked up and now there were cars slowing on the highway, little red brake lights blinking through the weather.

"I know she's mine," he said. "I know you named her after that song I wrote."

"We can still pretend she ain't," said Joelle. "No one would be the wiser. The resemblance works either way. You can go back down to Louisiana like nothing happened. You fought for us and you earned a way out."

He glanced at the rearview, and this time she held his gaze.

"You figure there's another way to go about it?" he asked.

"Well," she said. "I could use the help, if you're willing. I only have one condition if you wanna stick around."

"Just one?"

"One for now."

Delmore didn't answer at first. He thought he knew what it could be, but he didn't want to say the wrong thing. He didn't want to make a promise he couldn't keep.

Still, her silence drew it out of him.

"You don't want me drinking?" he said, finally.

"That ain't it."

"What then?"

"I don't want you to ever play that fuckin' song again," she said.

I Keep Coming Back Empty Handed

It was just before nightfall when my mother rushed through the front door and asked about the missing boy. She crowded me as I sat watching TV, a ring of keys clenched in one hand and the boy's flier in the other, searching my face like I was the one leading the effort, like I had all the answers somehow.

"Couldn't find him," I said. I could hear the exhaustion in my own voice. After a long day in the canyon, my face and neck badly sunburned, I didn't have the energy to give all the details. "We searched all afternoon, then another group took over. Half the canyon is still off-limits because of the fire."

"Maybe you should have joined the other group, too?"

"I was hungry," I said. "Janice from next door brought some kind of casserole for the volunteers but it had peas in it. I came home and made a sandwich instead."

"That poor kid is more important than a bad casserole, don't you think?"

She set the flier on the coffee table and unclasped her silver hoop earrings. The local news was coming on and a photo of the boy appeared over the newscaster's shoulder—the same photo as the flier. He was cradling a yellow Tonka truck and pointing at something off-camera, his bowl-cut hair askew. The newscaster detailed the wildfire and the evacuations that preceded the boy's disappearance. They ran videos of search parties marching through fields, parting the long dry grass with walking sticks, a dreary smoke hanging over the scene like some old war movie. I looked for myself in the video, but the clip ended quickly and they were onto the next story.

"I'll be there Sunday if they don't find him by then," said my mother. "God, I hope they do. I want you to search every day, understand? You don't have anything better to do until September."

"Well, the waves have been pretty good lately."

"Are you kidding me? The waves will come and go till the end of time, but this poor boy—"

She trailed off with her earrings cupped in her hand, watching the glow of the newscast without really paying attention. They'd moved on to Operation Desert Storm, and now the space over the newscaster's shoulder had been commandeered by Saddam Hussein's mustachioed grin. Her eyes got wet, and she sat beside me on the couch and put an arm around me.

"I'm glad you're safe," she said. "It could be anybody's kid out there. Sometimes you have to stop and count your blessings." She kissed the top of my head and rose again and started across the room to her bedroom. She stopped in the doorway and loosened her blue bank teller scarf, just watching me for a moment, then she shut the door and disappeared for the night.

I hadn't seen the new flier yet, so I picked it up and glanced over the details—the boy's height, the color of his eyes, the clothes he wore when he disappeared. They'd written a list of things he liked and places he was familiar with. I wondered what they'd say about me if I went missing, what it would be like to hear my name shouted from some half-scorched meadow over and over as the night folded in. I set the flier down, but after a few minutes I picked it up and read it again.

He likes yellow trucks, it said.

He likes to climb trees.

***

The search party gathered at sunrise.

We stood near the rim of the canyon where a narrow dirt path angled down along the oaks and redwoods. Someone had set up a table and the early volunteers were picking through boxes of donuts and pouring carafes of coffee and juice into paper cups. I was one of the first to arrive, but it wasn't because my mother had shooed me out of the house on her way to work. It wasn't the donuts, either. The day before, I'd met another volunteer named Danielle who was a grade above me. She'd started living with her grandparents and didn't know anyone in the neighborhood, and she had a lot of questions about the town and the school and what it was like to live here.

And I liked talking to her.

I spotted her as she came strolling down the trail alone. She waved to me and wandered over. Her sun-bleached hair reminded me of some of the surfer girls I'd met at the beach, even though I'd never seen her there. Her shirt bore the name of a gymnastics program from some Central Valley cow town.

"Hey, kid from yesterday," she said. "Any donuts left?"

"Bad news," I said, sweeping my hand over the table. "They're out of maple bars. I'm just gonna leave, to be honest. There's nothing left for me here."

She laughed, then caught herself.

An older woman threw a disapproving look as she poured the juice. Her eyes said *this is no laughing matter.*

Danielle leaned in close and whispered.

"I suspected you were in it for the donuts."

"Not just any donuts," I whispered back. "Maple bars."

A few minutes later we descended into the canyon with our canteens and walking sticks and reflective orange vests, calling the boy's name as we went. The sun slanted brightly through the redwoods, steaming what was left of the night fog from the long grasses. We poked at bushes and peered into hollow logs.

Danielle and I walked together, and she told me a little about her life in the Central Valley—but changed the subject when I asked about her family. I got the sense there was more to her leaving home than she was letting on. She laughed and smiled like a nervous habit, like a mask to hide something else. So I told her about surfing, about the little waves south of Santa Cruz when the tide goes out, how pods of dolphins sometimes swim beside you. I told her about the tide pools and the sea lions and the sharks that cruise beneath the old pier. It was all she wanted to talk about. She couldn't get enough.

By noon, we'd wandered far from the group. Danielle had spotted a herd of deer stepping through the scrub oak and we watched from the corpse of an old redwood that some previous wildfire had charred and hollowed.

"Maybe he was chasing deer," she said. "He could have broken his leg when he ran after them."

"Maybe." A squirrel scrabbled around the trunk with an acorn jawed tightly, watching with unblinking eyes. I tapped the trunk with my walking stick and it skittered away. "Maybe he climbed after a squirrel and got stuck in a tree."

"I guess that's a possibility," she said, looking up.

The redwood had sent new growth around the trunk before it withered, and we found ourselves inside a circle of redwood saplings. We called the boy's name with our heads tilted back, hands balled at our lips. A breeze came down the canyon smelling of wildfire smoke, and we listened for a response. Somewhere a raven clacked its beak. We circled the trunk, walking opposite directions—and then we were facing each other, standing close. I'd kissed a girl before, but just a peck. Something to say we'd done it and nothing more. But when I kissed Danielle there was something else there, and it didn't end with the two of us running away giggling, but with a long embrace and more kissing.

"I don't think we'll find him this way," she said.

"They can form another search party if they want to."

She laughed and pulled me onto the trail, and we followed the faint voices of the volunteers back through the canyon.

***

By the fifth day, a weariness had spread through the group. The afternoon crew trudged down the trail as the morning crew hiked out, each passing the other with grim nods and few words spoken. It felt more like a shift change at a coal mine than a search and rescue operation. I'd heard the boy's name so many times that my brain simply filtered it out. It became like a written word scrutinized too closely, the meaning lost, the lettering absurd. The lost boy was no match for the sensationalism of the Gulf War, and he garnered less time on the nightly news and soon disappeared from the front page of the local newspaper entirely.

I'd started walking Danielle to her grandparents' condominium in the afternoons after the searches. By now we were holding hands as we went, and I'd promised to take her to the beach so she could paddle out in the gentle mid-county waves with the dolphins. With her gymnastics training, I had no doubt she'd catch on quickly, and she teased that she'd be better than me by the time school started. She still hadn't told me why she'd left the valley, only that her mother had sent her, and the coast was a better place to grow up anyway.

We were turning the corner into her neighborhood when she spun the other direction and ran. I stood watching as she shouldered behind a row of tall hedges a half block down the road and vanished. The street looked unremarkable to me—quiet, no one about. I didn't know what to do, so I went slowly down the block and peered into the hedges to ask what was wrong. She sat there among the brambles and spider webs with her hands laced around her knees, eyes overflowing. She saw me and tried to smile, but it wasn't even passable—sort of a strange and disordered grin.

"The red truck," she said. "It's missing a tailgate. Do you see it?"

I glanced up and down the street.

"No red trucks—"

"You didn't even look." She said it like I'd betrayed her somehow, like there were two sides to whatever this was, and she couldn't decide whose side I was on. "Look harder. Go past my grandparents' house and tell me what you see."

I searched for something else to say. I must have taken too long, because she buried her face in her hands and shouted for me to *just go.* A car passed—an older model Nissan with sun blisters on the hood, a white-haired woman slouching behind the wheel. It was the only car on the road. I wandered past the beige condo and didn't find anything there, either. A pair of dragonflies flew into the scene and harried each other for a moment before zipping away. At the end of the road where it teed with the main boulevard, I spotted a pickup truck hooking left and melding into traffic, but it was far away, and I couldn't make out the color.

She flinched when I returned.

"Just me," I said.

"What did you see?"

"Nothing. Maybe a truck, but it was far away."

"What color?"

"I couldn't tell. Could've been red. It's gone now and the street's empty. Looks like the whole block hasn't come home from work yet."

I wedged into the small space, close enough to hold out my hand. Maybe she'd decided I was on her side after all, because she took it and slowly rose, wiping the webs from her face.

"Want to go somewhere with me?" she said. I thought maybe her eyes had flecks of green in them now, but it could have been the way the light played with the tears.

"Sure," I said. "I don't have to be home till sunset."

"You remember that old stump with the little circle of trees around it, the one way down in the canyon? While I was sitting here, I was thinking how peaceful it was. I was telling my grandmother about it and she called it a fairy circle. You ever hear that? *A fairy circle.* I want to go back there with you."

"You want to go now?"

She brushed another dusty web from her shirt.

"Unless you want to sit in these hedges all afternoon." Her fear was fading now—or maybe she'd forced it down by sheer will. "Just help me keep an eye on the road, will you?"

"The red truck?"

"Yeah, the red truck."

We avoided the main road, climbing over a jangly chainlink, then through the elementary school playground, the fields, and into the dark of the redwoods. She tried to apologize for what happened, but I told her not to. I wondered if it had something to do with her father, so I told her about my own father, how he'd gotten so many DUIs that he lost his license for good, and soon after, got so drunk he rode his ten-speed onto the freeway and caused an awful wreck. It wasn't something I ever talked about, and it felt strange telling the story. Strange, but also something of a relief to share it with her.

"He drove a big white van," I said. "Every time I see one, a part of me thinks it's him, even though he wrecked it years ago."

"Do you see him anymore?"

"He's still in jail for the freeway thing. Hasn't even had a trial yet. But yeah, I visit him sometimes."

"Must have been a bad wreck," she said.

"Bad enough to make the news. My mom and I would visit almost every day at first. Then once a week. I haven't seen him since Father's Day, and so far, that's the longest stretch."

It took us a half hour to hike across the canyon to the fairy circle. By then she'd told me it wasn't her father she was worried about, but her stepfather. She wouldn't tell me what he'd done, but it was bad enough that her mother sent her a few hundred miles away for her own good. She thought her stepfather was looking for her, but he didn't know where her grandparents lived—at least, she didn't think he did. As we sat in the cooling afternoon beneath the redwoods, our backs pressed to the dry summer soil, I finally understood why she felt so safe here, far from the anxious city streets.

"Let's plan to meet here if anything bad happens," I said. "Doesn't matter what it is. Maybe it's the red truck, maybe something else. Nobody will ever know this is our place."

She quietly agreed, squeezing my hand—but her voice sounded far away. She fixed on a small cloud drifting high above the canopy.

"What are you thinking about?" I asked her.

"I was thinking about the boy. How nobody stays lost forever. Sooner or later, someone will find him. Alive or dead. But I'm also thinking how soon enough maybe someone will find me, too—the wrong person."

"But you're not lost, you're hiding. That's a big difference."

"Is it? I don't know." She rolled onto her shoulder, touched my face with her fingertips. "They feel like the same thing."

***

"She's pretty," my mother told me. "Is she your—*girlfriend?*" She'd spotted Danielle and I holding hands on her way home from work and it was all she wanted to talk about. I'd heated a pot pie in the oven and was waiting for it to cool when she sat beside me at the dining table, grinning wolfishly, devouring every clue my face would reveal.

"Mom."

"Don't *mom* me. I have a right to know."

"I don't know—I guess she is. We didn't have a ceremony or anything."

"Such a romantic. Will she be at the search tomorrow? I'll be there, you know. I'd love to meet her, maybe show her some baby pictures."

"Please don't embarrass me."

She broke off a crispy piece of crust from the pot pie and wedged it into her left nostril with her eyes all screwed up.

"That's my job, hon."

"Stop it, oh my god that's gross," I said, waving her off. "But you should know, it's been depressing down there lately. Nobody thinks they're going to find him alive at this point. They don't come out and say it—but everyone just knows."

She took the crust and broke it apart in her hand.

"It's important to have hope, kiddo. Without hope, folks just give up—and that leads to all kinds of trouble. Go visit your father for a lesson on giving up. You won't even need to talk to him. Just watch him sit there in his sad little orange getup, waiting for his transfer to San Quentin—for the next ten years of his life to begin. That's what giving up does to you."

I flicked on the TV.

Tracers arcing over the Iraqi desert. Burning oil wells.

"He woke me up from a nightmare once," I said. We were both watching the TV, all the black smoke, army tanks half-buried in the sand. "I don't know if I ever told you. I guess I was crying in my sleep."

"Was he sober?"

"No, he'd been drinking. It was just before he went away."

"What did he say?"

"It was hard to understand him. He said something about how the real nightmare hadn't begun yet. How it's not something you can wake up from. He said we're born into a dream, and childhood is just a whir of color and fake holidays and funny things that don't matter much, and it's only when we wake up that we see the real nightmare underneath."

"Sounds like something he'd say."

"Is he wrong?"

She stood and went to the window, wringing her hands.

I wondered if she was thinking about the boy.

"Are you crying?" I asked.

"A little."

"Why?"

"It would hurt my heart if you thought life was a nightmare. I told you already. Even if you can't see the good in the world, you have to have hope that it's there. Otherwise, you'll never find it. You'll just give up like your father."

"I get it," I said. "But isn't there a difference between giving up and moving on? With this boy, everyone will start to grieve at some point. It wouldn't mean anyone gave up on him."

"Maybe. But let's say the boy is alive somehow. Maybe he's living off creek water and bugs and sleeping in a hollow log. To him, there's no difference if the neighborhood gave up or moved on. It's the same thing. That's what I've been trying to tell you. When you give up hope, you take it away from everyone else, too. Let the family decide what the difference is."

***

Next morning, we walked to the command post above the canyon and waited for the rest of the volunteers to arrive. Someone had updated the flier, and I looked over the new details—a birthmark, a missing front tooth. It had been ten days since the boy vanished, and while there were still plenty of volunteers, the crowd had thinned. This time there was a young deputy with a black and white search dog. She'd been focusing on another part of the canyon without luck, and now she was joining us on our section. The sight of the dog boosted the mood of the volunteers, and there was a buzz and chatter that hadn't been there since the first day.

But Danielle still hadn't come.

I stood looking up the trail, imagining her shuffling through the oak scrub with that complicated smile, turning the corner any minute now. My mother and I waited until the others disappeared, their voices fading below.

"You want to wait for her a while longer?" she said. With her homemade knit hat, orange vest, and basket full of snacks, my mother looked more like a wild mushroom hunter than anything else. "It's okay. Why don't you catch up later?"

"Yeah," I said. "I'll catch up."

I waited for Danielle another few minutes. It was still early and there was a thin gray mist hanging in the blackberry brambles, the raking sounds of birds in the dry leaves. I was about to give up when the deputy came running toward me with the dog at her heels, radio clacking and hissing. She yelled her call sign and location into the radio and passed without seeing me, like I wasn't even there. I asked if they'd found the boy, and she yelled back *no*, but didn't say anything else. I watched her climb into the patrol car at the top of the canyon and she sped away in a cloud of dust.

I don't know what drove me to follow the deputy, but even as she vanished down the main road toward the neighborhood, I continued after her—first jogging, then running—until I'd made it all the way down the hill just a block from Danielle's home. I couldn't untangle the urgent look on the deputy's face from the fact that Danielle hadn't shown, like they were connected somehow. She was all I ever thought about, and I had to know if she was in danger. A fire truck turned off her street as sheriff 's cruisers swerved in with lights and sirens. I stopped at the corner amid the ocean of blue and white lights, cops standing by their cars with rifles held to their chests.

Then I saw it, halfway down the block.

A red truck with a missing tailgate.

I inched toward the chaos of lights and uniforms. I knew I wasn't supposed to, but I did it anyway. I needed to know what was happening, where Danielle was in all of this. A middle-aged cop with a tight gray mustache spotted me and yelled to stay back. There were cops coming out of her house with graveyard faces, cops peering grimly from the second-story window. It was like the earth had cracked open and the center was filled with sad cops waiting to come shuffling out.

"I told you to *stay back*," said the gray-haired cop.

"My friend lives there," I said, and I thought I'd said it defiantly, like I didn't care what he wanted me to do, like I knew more than him.

But he could tell how scared I was, and he softened a little.

"Just let us do our job, kid," he said. "It's a bad scene."

I wanted to tell him about the red truck, how afraid it made Danielle. I wanted to tell him about her stepfather and how he wasn't supposed to know where she lived. I wanted to shout it to all the sad cops with their heads slowly shaking like they didn't know what to make of it.

But then I remembered our secret place.

Whatever happened here, I decided Danielle wasn't a part of it. She was too cautious to get caught in something like this.

She'd seen the red truck and ran off just in time—and all I had to do was go find her.

I ran through the neighborhood so fast that all the dogs barked in their yards when they heard me pass. I could still hear the sirens down below, and I imagined running past burning oil wells and mortar explosions in the Iraqi desert, missiles launching into the gunshot sky. I imagined Danielle not far ahead of me, crossing the elementary school and scaling the chainlink, descending the rooty, narrow trail where no red trucks could ever follow.

By the time I found the fairy circle, I'd run out of breath. I stood hunched with my hands on my knees, coughing out her name. I went staggering around the old stump and searched the redwoods along the little creek that trickled through the canyon. I called her name down every deer trail and rocky washout, and when she didn't answer, I kicked through the scrub toward the burn scar and went over the blackened ground until the trees rose above me like spent matchsticks and the air reeked of charcoal. In this ruined place, there were no birds or animals or flying bugs—just a cruel gray smoke that webbed among the trees like a hag's curse.

I stumbled along until soot darkened my shoes and pants and I no longer knew the direction home. My legs ached, everything felt sore. I wept under a barren oak tree until the sun rose high over the treetops. She was gone, and no one could help her. I knew that my father had been right all along, and why it had driven him so crazy. I saw the nightmare, now. I could still see the dream, too, but the colors faded fast and all the terrible things had come rushing in around it.

I looked down at my wrecked tennis shoes.

Under the scorched leaves was a spot of color.

I kicked at it—*a yellow toy truck.* It looked small and de-formed, little plastic wheels melted to the chassis like drops of candle wax.

I circled the tree, nudging the soil with the tips of my shoes.

Something lay above me, near the base of a long, arcing branch. Something dark and vaguely doll-shaped—but also blistered and lobed like a fungus. An awful, howling wind blew, the kind of sound only a dead forest could make, and I stood watching the thing, wondering. I tilted my head and palmed the tears from my eyes and looked again. What I thought at first were seeds now looked like a row of little brown teeth with one tooth missing—a grisly scowl pinned to a hairless, cindered head.

I slipped the flier from my pocket and unfolded it.

He likes yellow trucks, it said.

He likes to climb trees.

Dig Deep the Midnight Furrows

It was a hot Wednesday afternoon when Dean Brower came home to find his father drunk on the front porch, a bottle of Bud resting upright in his hands. He had his boots kicked up on the railing and his hat pulled over his eyes, shielding the late Tennessee sun. Beside him sat a folding table with a crowded ashtray and a half-eaten bologna sandwich.

"You awake, Pops?" Dean said. The old man gave no reaction save for the rise and fall of his breathing. "Pops? *Harvey*?"

The old man jolted, bottle tumbling from his hands. It made a hollow clatter against the porch boards and rolled in a lazy arc. He lifted his chin to see who was there with a hard squint, as if looking into the sun.

"Oh, hiya Deanie-boy," he said, when the recognition came. His voice had a quiet, joyful quality that could only have come six bottles deep into a twelve pack of beer.

"You on vacation?" said Dean. "Alfalfa looks like it's starting to bud." He tapped out a cigarette from a soft pack and torched it to life, the smoke whipsawing over his shoulder. "Little early for a party, ain't it?"

The old man shrugged and reached for the fallen bottle, but he lost his balance and fell square on his side. He tried to save himself by reaching for the folding table, but it toppled over him—an apocalypse of bologna and cigarette butts.

Dean took a pull from the cigarette and watched with mild amusement. A trio of barn flies had found the sandwich and were lapping at the mayonnaise like kittens. He hadn't seen his father this drunk since his mother had passed.

"Hope you were done with that sandwich, Pops," said Dean.

The old man was on his knees now, trying to get his feet beneath him. He saw the bread and meat and cigarette butts spilled over the porch boards and waved his hand dismissively.

"*Fuck the sandwich.* I got bigger problems."

Dean helped him up.

"You gonna tell me what's going on?"

"Them bankers won't quit, Deanie." He fished a smoke from Dean's shirt pocket and held it at the corner of his mouth without lighting it. "There was an adjustment or some fuckin' thing and now they want another couple grand a month. We ain't got it this time."

"What do you mean *we ain't got it?*"

"I mean we ain't got it. They sucked every last drop of blood. Had a bunch of them fuckers over here this morning while you were in class. Surveying the property, you know. Heard 'em talking about growing soybeans for the Chinese when they take over the farm."

"Lucky I wasn't here," said Dean. He had found the twelve pack and fished out a warm bottle, cracked the cap. "I woulda come after 'em with the swather."

The old man plucked the beer from his hands.

"Still ain't old enough to drink, Deanie."

Dean took the bottle back.

"You ain't sober enough to tell me what to do."

The old man looked him up and down. Not long ago the remark would have earned him an open palm across the cheek—or at least the threat of one.

"Christ, you're ornery like your mother was. But with a worse figure."

They drank and smoked in silence, watching the wind roll through the acres of alfalfa. Yellow buds marbled in the green. A turkey vulture appeared over the road, the dark form a sudden malignancy against the bright blue sky. The old man went to the little radio on the windowsill and flicked the dial to an AM country station and pointed the antennae toward some vague point on the horizon.

"Want me to call Vic and Lenny?" Dean asked.

"Nah," said the old man. "They're worse off. You're the only one of your brothers that turned out half-decent anyhow."

"So, what are we gonna do?"

"I'll get a job at the factory like everyone else."

"You're too old for that."

"What choice do I got, son?" His eyes got wet and the sight of it made Dean turn away. It was only the second time he had seen his father cry.

"How much you need?"

"More than you got."

"How much?"

"Shit, Dean. It'd take twenty grand, and that'll just buy us some time."

Dean took out his key ring and spun it around his finger. He squeezed his father's shoulder with the other hand. They stood that way for a moment, Dean twirling the keys like he was leaving but holding each other at arm's length all the while.

"I'll be back, Pops," said Dean, finally.

"Where you off to, then?"

"To see if I can scare up twenty grand."

***

Dean parked the old Chevy a block from the Sevier National Bank on East Main. The light over the foothills was beginning to change, and a dank mineral stench rose off the Little Pigeon River. The bank was a four-story brick and concrete palace, the kind of building you'd expect to house a museum or some minor branch of government, with Roman columns and letters notched into the brick facade. He made it through the doors thirty minutes before closing. There were ferns in all corners of the lobby and a brushed steel coffee table with shiny leather chairs at the center. The smell of stale coffee and floorwax hung in the air.

"Dean?" A young teller with black hair and a navy blue blazer ambled across the lobby toward him. "Dean Brower, what are you doing here?"

"That you, Cordelia?"

"I hope you're not here for me." She said it in a loud whisper, tossing a glance to the other tellers behind the partition to see if they were watching.

They were.

"Good evening to you as well," said Dean.

"I'm at work, Dean. I can't have guys come calling for me on the clock, even a good-looking guy like you. Unless you got an account here. Then it's business."

Dean watched her with a slight grin. Her eyes were heating up with one eyebrow raised, hip pitched to one side.

"I got an account here," he said. "But it's the loan I'm wondering about. Pops says they're fixin' to take the farm and I wanna know how to stop it."

Cordelia looked him up and down. "This ain't about you and me?"

"Nope. I heard you was seeing Jake Barlow."

"Jack Barlow. Jake's his cousin."

"Well?"

"We broke up when he left for basic training."

"I see."

"But that ain't why you came?"

"It's about the loan, like I told you."

She softened, tossed another glance to the teller line.

"All the bankers went home for the day. But I tell you, a lot of old boys been coming in this week and last. Hollering about their loans, same as you. Guess they been hiking them rates."

The walls of the bank were crowded with old black and white portraits and Dean stood gazing up at them. Gray-haired aristocrats with fancy jewelry and little white dogs on their laps. Bronze plaques heralding the names of the exalted.

"Who're all them assholes?"

Cordelia looked. "The owners' forebears. The Whitakers and the Buchanans."

"Owners of the bank?"

"Well, most are dead, but the family still owns it."

"They been makin' money off farmers like us for generations. Looks like we been in the wrong business all along."

"I work here, dummy. *You're* in the wrong business."

"I'd never work indoors."

"Well, I got Blue Cross and a 401k."

"That mean you're buying dinner tonight?"

Cordelia gave Dean another once over. Her expression had taken an amused quality. She unfolded her arms and slipped her cell phone from her back pocket, gave it a few swipes and put it back. It looked like she was trying to make a decision but having trouble with it. She folded her arms and chewed her cheek, eyes heating up again.

"I'm off in ten minutes," she said.

"I'll bring the truck around."

"You're a good-looking sonofabitch, Dean Brower."

"You told me that already."

***

They sat on the open tailgate with a six pack between them and watched the headlights blinking along the highway. The moon was up, constellations lumbering along their celestial arcs. Dean had parked the Chevy beneath a pine tree that overlooked a feed store and the town cemetery. He had the radio tuned to his father's favorite country station and Merle Haggard was singing about being a lonesome fugitive.

"So, you gonna tell me what I gotta do?" Dean said.

"We're two beers deep and sittin' in the back of your truck under the stars," said Cordelia. She put her hand on his thigh and slid it up the inside of his jeans. "I'd say you done enough."

Dean smiled wide enough to catch the moonlight in his teeth.

"I was talking about the loan."

"You just like me for my professional expertise?"

"Isn't that what women want?"

"Sometimes. But we can put a pin in it for now."

Dean drew her close and they kissed for a long while. He ran his fingers up the back of her neck and spoke softly in her ear.

"I just need help, baby. You're the only one that can help us."

Cordelia pulled away and guzzled the rest of the beer. She set the empty bottle in the cardboard carrier and belched softly into the crook of her arm.

"I'm just a teller, Dean," she said. She had now taken the tone of somber counselor, albeit with a prominent slur on the consonants. "But from what I hear, they make more money on the foreclosure than the loan. Anytime you move a property there's costs and fees and commissions and new loans to be had. Them bankers don't make money unless there's a transaction. What I'm saying is if you throw enough money at 'em, they'll go away. Otherwise, they'll keep shaking the tree."

"I just ain't got that kind of money, Delia."

"Well, it ain't up to me."

Dean cracked another beer and shot the cap in the direction of the cemetery with a snap of his fingers.

"Shit," he said. "I bet all them dead Buchanans and Whitakers got enough jewelry buried with 'em to pay off everybody's loan. Just sitting in the dirt, doing nothing."

"Now hold on a minute," said Cordelia. She pulled the last beer from the carrier and opened it. "Is this the part of the story where Dean Brower becomes a grave robber?"

"Hell. I'd dig up one of them old ladies if it paid up the loan. Way I see it, our farms are rotting away inside them dead bankers' coffins." He rummaged through the loose tools in the back of the truck. When he stood again, he was holding a work-worn shovel, one hand on the grip and the other at the collar of the spade. "Want me to take you home first?"

Cordelia didn't answer right away. She took another pull from the bottle and sloshed what remained as if judging how much was left.

"Can we get more beer first? This ain't typically how I spend my Wednesday nights."

"There's a half bottle of whiskey under the seat."

"That'll do."

***

Dean stood before a granite obelisk, pasting the inscription with the beam of a small Maglite.

"This one says Whitaker," he said. He went to the next grave and looked it over. "This one's even fancier. Also Whitaker."

"Here's a Buchanan," said Cordelia. She was teetering over the ground with the whiskey bottle in one hand and a dead flashlight in the other. She slapped the flashlight against her thigh and the light sputtered forth a paltry brown glow. "And here's another one. I think we're in the right spot. If you're gonna do this, you better stick to these here older graves."

"Why's that?"

"I heard they seal 'em up in concrete now. Saw it on TV."

"I knew you were the right woman to bring along."

Dean tested the ground with the shovel.

"Pretty soft here," he said. He pressed the spade deeper with the heel of his boot. "Kill that light so nobody'll see us from the road."

He dug by moonlight, the shovel ticking at the soil with the sound of an old clock. The hole grew slowly, and he descended with it through the roots and stones. It wasn't as easy to undig a grave as it looked in the movies—the deeper he got, the harder it was to excavate the dirt. His shoulders ached as he pitched each shovel-load at the night sky.

He called up from the hole. "See anybody on the road?"

"Not a soul," said Cordelia. "It's a little spooky though."

"Hand me down some of that whiskey," he said. "I need to wet my throat." She obliged, and he took the bottle and drank. He wiped the sweat from his forehead and drank again. "I think I'm getting close now."

"It ain't a crime to watch you?"

"If we get caught, I'll tell them you tried to talk me out of it."

"You better. Never had a date like this before."

Dean stabbed the shovel straight down and it replied with a hollow knock.

"Just wait, 'cause it just got even spookier. Bring the light."

It didn't take long to clear the dirt from the top of the casket. Dean had to dig footholds in the walls of the grave so he could pull open the lid. When he finally got it open, he hollered and covered his mouth with his hand.

"Oh my God," said Cordelia, wagging the light over the coffin. She was decidedly drunk now and her voice cracked with astonishment. "There's a real dead old lady in there."

Dean stood with his mouth covered, the reek of death welling from the coffin.

"What'd you reckon we'd find?"

"I don't know," she said, and she repeated it several times, maundering and staring down at the hole. "I wasn't confident you'd get this far, to be honest."

Dean squatted atop the corpse, looking it over with the flashlight pinched between his shoulder and his ear like he'd come from a long line of graverobbers. An eyeless mummy gazed back. Greyish arms withered to the bone. The jaw had fallen open and there was a large white wig spooled around the skull with the mesh decoupled from the scalp. Around the throat lay two gold necklaces with gemstone pendants. Matching earrings nestled in the rot. Dean gathered the jewelry and handed it up to Cordelia, who immediately donned them as her own.

"Check the fingers for rings, dummy," she called down.

Dean felt the hands, fingers like vegetable roots. He slipped off two diamond rings and pushed them deep into the toe of his front pocket. Something else caught his eye. At the foot of the casket was another jumble of bones shrouded in white hair. Beneath it, a sparkling collar studded with gemstones.

"Ain't that something," said Dean. "One of them dogs is buried here."

"Ain't surprised. Them dogs are in all the portraits."

"This one got a fancy collar, though. Shit. Bankers' dogs are richer than most people in this town." He tossed up the collar and closed the coffin lid. Cordelia helped him climb out of the hole and they looked over the jewels in a state of wonder.

"How much you reckon this is all worth?" Cordelia asked.

"No telling. There's a few pawn shops in Knoxville that'll give me cash, though. We sold off some of my mom's jewelry there after she died. Pops said we got a good price."

Cordelia took the collar and clasped it around her neck. She looked like an Egyptian pharaoh, gemstones winking in the moonlight. She twirled in a clumsy circle and gave a bow.

"What do you think?" she asked. "Does it suit me?"

"Maybe, If you're trying to look like a rich banker."

"Better than a *dead* banker."

Dean laughed. "Nothing's better than a dead banker."

They splashed booze over the grave to anoint the desecrated plot and they made the sign of the cross in the air with their fingers. After Dean shoveled the dirt back into the hole, they screwed against an oak tree with the stolen jewelry chiming against their bodies and the calls of whippoorwills and night toads burbling down the tree-lined draws of the Appalachian foothills.

***

Dean was eating fried eggs and grits at Mel's Diner when two large men in wrinkle-free shirts and clip-on ties approached and asked if he was Dean Brower. When he nodded, they asked if they could sit down.

"It's a free country, more or less," said Dean.

The one that did the talking was a sweaty hogjowled man named Searcy, and the other was a smaller replica of Searcy who had introduced himself as Brian. Searcy laid a leather badge holder on the table and unfolded it while he sized Dean up with his eyes.

"I'm with the FBI, Dean," said Searcy. He kept flicking his eyes to Dean's plate as if he hadn't yet eaten and was longing for a hearty breakfast. "Brian here is with FINCEN."

Dean took another bite and chewed, smiling at the two men. He sipped from a ceramic coffee mug and wiped his mouth politely with a paper napkin.

"It's a pleasure," said Dean. "Did you say you were with Vincent? I don't know who that is."

"Not *Vincent*," said Brian. "FINCEN. We investigate financial crimes."

"Well, I'd be happy to help, fellas," said Dean. "Thing is, my finances ain't much to talk about."

The pair looked at one another and the smaller man flicked at a tablet and set it beside Dean's plate. Dean's eyes fell over the image on the screen with fleeting interest.

"Recognize that man?" asked Brian.

"Looks like me doing some bank business," said Dean. He poked at the remaining egg with the tines of his fork and dipped a corner of the toast in the yolk. "That a crime?"

Brian flicked the screen, revealing a succession of photos of Dean engaged in various transactions with different timestamps. "You went to five different Sevier National Bank branches and deposited eight thousand dollars toward your father's business loan with each transaction. That's forty grand in a single day. All cash."

"I suppose the loan needed paying."

Searcy slipped his ID into his jacket pocket. "See, this kind of thing sets off a bunch of alarms. We got protocols in place to prevent money laundering. You in some kind of trouble, son?"

"Depends on the day and who you ask."

"Drugs?"

"No sir."

"We get a lot of meth and heroin cases out this way."

"I heard. Coffee is the only drug I need."

"Using drugs is one thing. Selling is another."

"None of that, gentlemen," said Dean. "I stay away from drugs."

Searcy rolled his head atop his pink neck until the vertebrae popped.

"We're not here to arrest you, Dean. We'd just like to get to the bottom of things. You sell any farm equipment lately? A few tractors, maybe?"

"Not lately."

"So where'd you get the money?"

Dean pushed his breakfast around the plate and was deliberating a response when a young deputy entered and made his way to Dean's table. Dean recognized him from high school.

"Hey there, Dean," said the cop.

"Hey there, Willard."

"I saw your truck out front and wondered if I could ask you about something, but I see you got company."

"These old boys don't mind," said Dean.

The men shrugged.

"We're looking for witnesses. Somebody dug up a grave at the county cemetery. Some rich old lady, I guess. They might've made off with some jewelry. Mr. Denny at the feed store thought maybe he saw you up on the hill last week drinking beer with a girl." He held up a phone and showed a picture of a grave with freshly dug soil spilled over the plot. "See anything out of the ordinary while you was up there?"

The feds eyed each other.

Dean slipped his wallet out and laid a twenty on the table. He set the coffee mug atop the bill and rose, brushed the crumbs from his lap.

"I'd love to help, Willard. Just that I really got to get on."

Searcy slapped his palms flat on the table, hard enough to make the syrup glass rattle.

"Now hold on a minute," he said. "What's this about a grave robbery?"

Dean scooted from the booth and made a few cool steps toward the door before breaking into a full sprint. He got to his truck and fishtailed onto the highway in a typhoon of brown dust before anyone else had even made the parking lot.

***

It was mid-September when the old man came stiff-legged through the buckeyes with a cooler swinging from one hand and a walking stick in the other. He stopped and looked about, his nose taking on the smell of woodsmoke that carried in the breeze. Ravens and warblers called from the overhead branches.

Dean appeared in the clearing with an old hunting rifle in his hands. His face had thinned and from his jaws hung a wiry black beard.

"That you, Pops?"

"Wish I'd thought to check here sooner," said the old man.

"Our old hunting camp."

"Don't I know it."

They hugged and slapped each other on the back. The old man opened the cooler and handed Dean a cold beer.

"Thought I wasn't old enough yet," said Dean.

"Hell. You look damn near thirty all of a sudden."

"I'm sorry for runnin' off, Pops. Sorry for what I done. Them bankers got me angry is all."

"You stirred up some shit, son."

Dean tipped the bottle and drank. He made a satisfied *ahh* and looked the bottle over with admiration.

"How long's it been?" said Dean. "I lost track out here."

"Reckon it's been a month."

"Feels about right."

"You eating okay?"

"Rabbits and squirrels, mostly."

"You can starve eating rabbits."

"Been eating the giblets too."

"Used to be an apple orchard down the way."

"I borrowed a few."

Dean led his father to a campfire where a thin gray finger of smoke coiled and dissipated into the fir canopy. Overhead were pink cutlets of rodent meat dangling from a branch. The dry leaves around the campfire had been worn to a fine dust with all his worried pacing. He sat on a log and poked at the coals with a long stick, his eyes hard and weary like some hopeless castaway.

"The Sheriff called me yesterday," said the old man.

"How is he, then?"

"Son, you stirred up more shit than you know."

"That so?"

"Yeah, *that's so*. He's gonna ask the DA not to throw the book at you, but you gotta help him clean up the mess you made."

"What mess?"

"I ain't mad at you. In fact, I'm impressed."

"Ain't like you to beat around the bush, Pops."

The old man folded his arms and looked at the sky, building the words carefully in his mind. Dean thought maybe the old man had aged since he'd seen him last, and it gave him an uneasy feeling. Maybe it was the same feeling he'd given the old man.

"They took over the fuckin' bank, Deanie."

"Who took over the bank?"

"A bunch of farmers. Dale Hetthouse is one of 'em. Also, the Smiths from Boyd's Creek. They heard about all that bank trouble you got yourself into and it inspired them. They gone and done the same."

"I sure as shit didn't take over no bank."

"Well, they dug up some graves just like you supposedly done. Only this time they hauled the coffins to the bank in Sevierville. Dragged 'em right through the front doors. Crazy bastards. All of them been holed up inside for a couple days, making demands about their loans. The sheriff wants you to talk to 'em in exchange for leniency. They look up to you now, I suppose. Somehow you became their patron saint of dipshittery—no offense to you, Deanie."

Dean offered a laugh, but it was brief.

"What about them feds?"

"What about 'em?"

"There's feds involved."

"Shit, son. I don't know about all that. But you'd better take this deal. Gonna be cold enough to freeze the tits off a steel cow in a few weeks. You can't stay here forever."

"I could make it through the winter if you brought me a tent and some blankets."

The old man rested on a log and gave the measly fire a long, thoughtful look.

"See, there was this wealthy silk merchant once," he said, scratching at his beard as if the story could be conjured there. He'd often slip allegories into conversations without warning, but this wasn't one Dean had heard before. "He married a beautiful young woman but ate and drank way too much on his wedding night. He'd spared no expense on booze and food, you see. So when it came time to do the deed, he farted so loud you could hear it for miles around. It echoed through the city streets and woke up sleeping babies. I mean, this was the King Kong of farts. The merchant gets so embarrassed that he skips town and disappears for years. He hides in the woods, kinda like what you're up to."

"I think I see where this is going," said Dean.

"Just let me finish. After ten years or so, he figures it's been long enough, so he wanders back into town, and as he does, he overhears this little girl asking her mother about the night she was born. You know what the mother says? She says, *oh little one, you were born on the night of the silk merchant's mighty fart!*" The old man wheezed out the last few words and bared his yellow teeth. "You see, son—ain't nobody gonna forget the shit you pulled. Not in this little town. So you might as well come back home and face the damn music."

Dean held his stomach as if his father's words had triggered a hunger cramp, and he eyed the sick-looking meat hanging over him like so many severed tongues.

"Maybe I'll come with you after all."

The old man nodded happily and slapped his hand on Dean's knee.

"We don't have to go directly," he said. From the cooler he found a pair of Ziploc bags with bologna sandwiches inside and he tossed one to Dean and cracked another beer for himself. "Figured you'd be hungry."

Dean unsheathed the sandwich and pressed a third of it into his mouth at once. When he was done chewing, he wiped the mayonnaise from his lips with the back of his hand and said: "I could eat a whole goddamn hog between two slices of bread."

***

The parking lot at the Sevier National Bank on East Main was jammed with police cars and there were cones and emergency tape barring entrance to the lot on all sides. A large police van had parked along the road and a SWAT team was staging there with tactical gear. An autonomous rover jerked back and forth on the sidewalk and a news chopper circled overhead. When Dean and his father stepped out of the truck, they were greeted by the sheriff and two of his lieutenants. The sheriff was a lanky man with a practiced smile and cool demeanor. He offered his hand and they both shook it.

"Damn, son," said the sheriff. "You look like a bona fide fugitive. Somebody needs to call Hollywood."

Dean looked about the scene. He had never seen so many cops in his life.

"I heard maybe you needed my help," he said.

The sheriff tucked his thumbs in his belt and squinted thoughtfully at the bank as a fisherman might gaze over a river.

"Them boys inside the bank have some demands, Dean. They want us to drop charges for your little misadventure at the county cemetery, among other things. And I'm willing to do it, if you'd help bring 'em to their senses."

"How you reckon I do that?"

"Go in and talk, that's all. Tell them boys I'm taking care of you, and I'd be friendly and appreciative if they came out smiling so we can put this all behind us. Lord knows they won't listen to me."

"What about them loans? We all been getting screwed."

"Do I look like a motherfuckin' banker to you?"

"No sir."

"It ain't up to me. All I can do is all I can do." He looked to his lieutenants, and they confirmed this with obsequious nods.

"Well," said Dean. "I'll see about it, then."

"Damn right you will, son. You see the SWAT team over there? They're fixin' to kick some ass. And that's what you call a *euphemism*. These boys train all year and they're lucky to get one or two callouts. In the old days we'd be dragging out dead bodies by now, but times are changing, and we got to be friendly about it first. Now get on."

Dean ducked the emergency tape and crept across the lot to the bank entranceway. The large glass doors loomed overhead, and he could see figures moving about inside. When he got close enough, the door parted and a bushy-haired kid in overalls came halfway out and waved him in with a goofy smile. He thought maybe he was his old friend Boyd's cousin. Dean took a final look over his shoulder. It looked like every cop in the county was watching him.

He took a breath and walked through the front doors.

The scene inside the bank was like something out of the Book of Revelation. A mutiny of damned souls from some forgotten district of Hell. The farmers were piss-drunk and getting drunker by the second. Someone had pried open the registers and carpeted the lobby with cash. One man had stapled hundred-dollar bills to his overalls so he looked like a commercial pitchman for some local auto dealership, save for the urine stains down his trouser leg. Dean scavenged a few hundred dollars and folded the stack neatly into his shirt pocket, noting how every corner of the bank held a worse sight than the last. Four grim coffins lay exhumed in the center of the lobby, and the corpses had been made to sit in the bank chairs as if they'd perished while waiting for their numbers to be called. They sat eyeless and shrunken in their grave rags, cave-like mouths gaping at the tin ceiling. The portraits had all been pulled from the walls with holes cut into the mouths and sketched on the faces were cartoon dicks with fountains of ejaculate.

When the group saw Dean, they greeted him with jubilant howls and lifted him into the air. They shouted his name as though he were their long-awaited savior, a robin hood returned to the ghettos of Nottingham. They carried him in a swarm of hands and reeking faces to the teller partition where he stood over the adoring maniacs in a state of shock and wonder.

The room stilled. They waited for him to speak.

Dean looked to the window at the scene outside. The SWAT van idled on the road. The sheriff stood impatiently in his tan and green uniform. He looked over the corpses arranged on their chic leather chairs. The grand portraits with their little dogs and their dickhole mouths. He bent down, motioned to a shovel leaning against a nearby wall. The bushy-haired kid fetched it for him and Dean took it and quietly looked it over, contemplating everything he had set in motion that night in the cemetery.

His eyes flicked once more over the crowd and then he stood and pressed the shovel into the air like some triumphant mountaineer atop a summit.

"Dig deep!" he shouted.

The room erupted in a frenzy. It was the phrase they had all wanted to hear but hadn't quite anticipated. A rallying cry in two little words. They shouted the words and he shouted them back, the cries booming and echoing in the immense vault of the room.

"Dig deep!" he called again, his shovel held high. "From now on, every farm we lose is one more dead banker we'll set up right here in the lobby."

"Dig deep!" was their reply.

Outside, the lights of the patrol cars strobed against the front doors. The chopper trundled in some unseen part of the sky. Radios clicked and call signs repeated.

The tan uniforms took their positions.

The sheriff gave his command.

Mercy, Mercy

Everyone says how safe this town was in the *good ol' days.*

You hear it wherever you go.

'You could leave your front door unlocked,' they say. *'People used to smile and say good morning when they passed you on the street.'* I heard someone going on about it just last week at the little produce market on South Main. Ice cream trucks and flower parades. Church on Sundays. Like we were all trapped in a sappy television show, gabbing to the mailman about how good the weather was and how long it might last.

But I remember the good ol' days much differently.

I remember when Rodney Langaniere killed all those kids back in '72.

***

I was living in a studio apartment a block or two from downtown, near the auto body shops and the used car joints. It wasn't a bad neighborhood, but I never left my door unlocked—and nobody smiled when they walked by. It was a working neigh-borhood, and everyone came and went on a schedule. From the little window over my sink, I could see the railroad tracks that brought redwood lumber from the north coast and strawberries up from the riverlands of the Pajaro Valley. On some nights, when the tide was low and the fog rolled in early, I could smell the sea as if the waves were slipping right past my front door.

I kept busy, working up the highway at the cement plant during the day, and picking up bartending shifts downtown on the weekends. I even made enough money to put some away. In the rainy season, the nights passed slowly and peacefully—an old fishing town longing for the good ol' days, just like now. But when the weather grew warm, Pacific Avenue swelled with wealthy day trippers from the South Bay, looking for cool ocean breezes and easy local girls. Tourists and locals never mix, espe-cially at last call when the night's fortunes were laid bare and the winners and losers were sorted and counted. I'm not a big guy, but I broke up plenty of fights over women, pride, dart games, whatever.

It was after closing time on one of those rowdy full moon summer nights in 1972 that Rodney Langaniere changed our little town forever—and it was also the night I met Mercy Dixon, the girl who was carved from the moon.

***

She screamed at me the moment I reached my front door.

Doing shift work at a cement plant, you get used to sudden noises, but goddamn, that scream stilled the blood in my veins. The house keys clattered at my feet, and I wheeled around to see this raven-haired woman, not more than twenty, shrieking in her nightgown like some kind of specter, bone-white fingers mussing and tearing at her hair. She stood just a few feet away, like she'd floated up behind me somehow, eyes walled in her sockets so all you could see were the white parts.

"Hey, hey, *it's all right.*" I said it over and over, fingers tapping the air even though it wasn't helping. Truth is, I didn't know if anything was all right or not—and by the sound of it, one of us was clearly wrong. By now, windows were lighting up in the neighborhood, and it sounded like every dog in the city was barking and howling. A part of me wanted to open the door, lock it behind me, and wait till someone else sorted it out. But the other part—the part that always makes things worse—wanted to help somehow. "What's wrong? Are you hurt? *Should I call the police?*"

It felt absurd, like playing twenty questions with a ghost.

Another woman called up from the street—an older and less agitated one by comparison—and she hurried up the driveway with a crocheted blanket draped over her arm. She was saying *mercy, mercy, mercy*—I was honestly thinking the same thing—but when she drew near, I realized it was the young woman's name and not an appeal to her humanity. Mercy took the blanket and gathered it close to her body and her screaming fell to a mewling whimper.

"I'm so sorry," said the older woman. She wore her thick gray hair pulled back in a loose ponytail and her spectacled eyes were kind and apologetic. "She must have given you quite a fright."

My instinct was to play it down, but the situation called for candor.

"I think your daughter owes me a new pair of pants."

"It's the moon," she said, as if it somehow made sense.

"The moon?"

"It fascinates her. On clear nights like this, when the moon is full or nearly full, she wanders off. She likes to follow it. And on foggy nights when she can't see the moon at all, she'll go searching for it. Like a lost cat."

"If I had the moon, I would've handed it over," I said.

"An old man used to live here. Mr. Hudspeth. He was kind to Mercy. I don't think she's accepted his passing. Her screams may be an expression of grief."

"Hudspeth, huh?" I still got mail addressed to him sometimes, so that part checked out. "She's going to be okay? You don't need me to call anyone?"

The woman led Mercy back to the street the way someone consoles the grief-stricken.

"She'll be fine," she said. "I'll come back tomorrow and leave my number in case it happens again. We only live a block away."

I gave another wave, locked the door behind me, and went straight to the liquor cabinet without taking my shoes off.

***

I didn't get out of bed until noon the next day, which was typical after a late shift at the bar. Sunday was my cleaning day, and I spent most of the afternoon tidying up the studio. Laundry, dishes, vacuuming. I always listened to loud music when I cleaned, and just as I was switching Led Zeppelin's second album for their fourth, I heard a knock at the door.

The older woman from last night stood holding a bottle of wine and an orange Tupperware container, which I hoped was full of cookies. She had a grandmotherly way about her, but I also had the sense she had aged in a hurry and wasn't quite as old as she seemed. Age has a way of hitting the fast-forward button when you're faced with more troubles than you can handle.

"Just something for last night," she said. "For your inconvenience."

"It was no inconvenience," I said. "You really didn't have to."

She insisted, and I felt the neighborly thing to do was invite her in for coffee. If it were any other day, maybe I wouldn't have. But my apartment was clean, and I was still curious about what the hell happened last night. I also offered wine, and she agreed that she'd rather have something stronger than coffee. She said her name was Sandra Dixon, and that she was a professor of English Literature up at the state college. She'd lived in the neighborhood ever since her husband and her only daughter died in a boating accident ten years ago. She watched me carefully when she said it, and I was gullible enough to take the bait.

"You trying to tell me your daughter's a ghost?"

"In a way, she is." She took a long sip from her glass and considered the wine thoughtfully. "After the accident, the Harbormaster found her floating in the bay and revived her. He won an award for it and everything. It was wintertime and the water was very cold. They say that's how it was possible to bring her back from the dead. Her father wasn't so lucky."

"How long was she—"

"About an hour. Maybe more. I'm lucky to have her back, but she's never been the same. Her father used to sing a song about a girl who was carved from the moon, and it's one of the few things she remembers. She thinks she belongs to the moon, or maybe it belongs to her. Either way, it's become a part of her identity."

"Does she talk at all?"

"Oh, she talks—but it's out of the blue. You could ask a thousand questions and never get a response. Next thing you know she's reciting Emily Dickinson."

"Why Emily Dickinson?"

"Why not Emily Dickinson? I told you I teach English Lit. Mercy writes her own poetry, too. She's quite talented—and that's not just her mother talking." Sandra gestured to the Tupperware container. "I left a slip of paper on top of the cookies with my phone number. If Mercy wanders your way again, just call. No need to stand there and let her scream at you. We really should look out for each other. I'm sure by now you've heard what happened to those kids over on Cedar Street?"

I gave a pitiful blank look.

"I'm surprised—you must have passed the scene on the way home last night," she said. "You didn't hear the shots?"

"The shots?"

Sandra Dixon poured herself another glass and filled me in.

***

It turned out Mercy Dixon's banshee routine wasn't the most terrifying thing to happen in the neighborhood that night. Three college students—all from the state college—were shot and killed in a downtown parking garage sometime after two in the morning. The oldest victim was a psych major named Logan Barnes who'd stayed in town for a summer job operating carnival rides at the Boardwalk. His friend Todd Willis, also among the dead, worked at the bowling alley nearby. The third and youngest victim was Logan's girlfriend, a nineteen-year-old coed named Janice Balco. Balco had just won a statewide poetry contest for a poem about whale migrations and her chapbook was on display in the window of the local bookstore. She was a student of Sandra Dixon, and that's how Sandra got the news so fast. The only detail the PD would disclose to the papers was that they all died instantly, which everyone assumed was a euphemism for execution.

***

The thing about murders in small towns is they create an instant paralysis. The streets grow quiet, tourists keep their distance. Police cruisers snake through the neighborhoods with search-lights panning from one side of the street to the other. Then, as the days stretch into weeks, the scapegoating sets in.

"It's the hippies," said Tom, my cement plant supervisor. He was an old wiry-haired local with gnarled hands who found a way to pepper his hatred of hippy culture into every conversation. I wore my hair pulled back in a ponytail back then, and I couldn't help but think some of the vitriol was directed at me. "Ever since that damn college opened for business, the town's been on a downward spiral. I say shut it down and run those freaks out on a rail."

Down at the bar, other crackpot theories thrived.

One of my regulars, a drunk salmon fisherman named Burt Salles, announced to the bar: "Dollars to donuts, it's them lettuce pickers from Watsonville. Bet they're talkin' about it right under our noses—and who could understand them? Gibberin' in ES-PAN-YOL."

I poured out his drink and pointed to the door.

One thing I could never stand was a bigot, and in those days, even the quiet bigots grew loud.

***

A month passed without an arrest, and just when the town's collective anxiety seemed to tick down a notch, the local newspaper slathered fresh buckets of ink onto a brand-new headline.

TWO DEAD IN NORTH COAST SHOOTING

I heard it from Sandra first. She intercepted me as I was pulling into the driveway after my cement shift, newspaper in her hands. She followed me all the way to my front door, filling me in on the new murders. This time, her eyes grew wet.

"Two more young people," she said. Her shoulders slumped with grief. "A couple, this time, camping on the beach near

Waddell Creek. The article says a beachwalker found them in the morning. Don't you work there at the cement plant?"

The way she said it almost sounded like an accusation.

"Not quite that far," I said. "Waddell Creek is near the county line. I never get up that far unless I'm driving straight through to the city. Were they both killed the same way?"

Sandra nodded grimly. She lifted her bifocals and knuckled the tears from her eyes. The news clearly hit her hard, and in this way she reminded me of my paternal grandfather. He was stoic, with a steel backbone. Past a certain age, however, he'd break down upon hearing the slightest tragedy. When I asked him why, he'd tell me tragedies were supposed to be upsetting, and if you didn't feel the loss in the pit of your stomach, you didn't really know what life was worth.

"Both were shot, yes," said Sandra. "While they lay in their sleeping bags, under the stars. It would be romantic if it wasn't so damn terrifying. I sure hope they were asleep when it happened."

"Maybe the first victim was, but the second would've woken with a start."

"Oh god, I suppose you're right."

I studied Sandra for a moment. She was lingering in the doorway as if she wanted to ask me something, trying to work up to it.

"I haven't lost your number, Sandra. I'll be sure to call if I see Mercy wandering around at night. We have to look out for each other, like you said."

It was the reassurance she was looking for.

"Thank you. I'm a heavy sleeper, and she can be so quiet. I had a big noisy deadbolt installed last week, but she's a bit of an escape artist. You know, the first shooting could have been a fluke, but now it feels like someone is hunting the young people in town. It's honestly all I think about."

"You're not alone," I said. "We're all worried about it."

It wasn't a lie—the whole town was on edge. It's all anyone wanted to talk about. The newspaper stands were empty by eight o'clock every morning and re-filled by nine. Maybe it was the contrarian in me, but I just wasn't as concerned as everyone else. I sensed paranoia everywhere I went, and it left me feeling sour. I had to deal with guys like Burt Salles and my supervisor Tom, and dozens of others with one dumb opinion after another. I was tired of all the fear and scapegoating and endless conspiracy theories.

But I sure didn't mind the empty streets.

Sometimes, after my dayshift, I'd come home and shower, then pour a pint of bourbon into my grandfather's old army canteen and walk three short blocks to the municipal wharf. Halfway down the rickety crossboards was a greasy deli window called Stagnaro Brothers that served fried fish sandwiches on sourdough with a magical garlic aioli for a measly buck. On a typical summer night, there'd be throngs of tourists crowding the wharf rails. Toddlers with ice cream-stained bellies. Striped umbrellas and beach towels dotting every inch of shoreline. But that summer, I had the entire coast to myself. Sometimes I'd bring a little Panasonic radio and sit at the end of the wharf with a fish sandwich and bourbon, listening to the college rock station as the great sparkling bay swallowed the sun and the first stars peeked shyly over the water. Don't get me wrong, I wasn't rooting for all the death and heartache. Five dead kids is a tragedy by any measure. I could feel the loss in the pit of my stomach just like my grandfather would have. But he also taught me to make the best of a bad situation, and that's exactly what I thought I was doing.

Looking back, however, had my grandfather been around, he would have thrown me a wizened look, clicked his tongue like a cowboy, and said, *you're pressing your luck, Jacky-boy.*

***

I'd passed out on a wharf bench and was shuffling home through dense coastal fog when I heard gunshots. Five, maybe six in a row. I told myself it was something else. *Anything else.* A car backfiring, or fireworks—it was July, after all, and it was common to hear kids setting off cherry bombs straight through August. But deep down, I knew. And when the screaming started, I thought of Mercy Dixon. The commotion was coming from my left, where the train tracks forked between Washington Street and continued northbound to Davenport.

I stood and listened. I didn't know what time it was. Midnight, at least. Maybe later.

Another scream came tearing out of the fog. A beastly shriek—*a woman fighting for her life.* I crept closer and saw a Dodge sedan parked beneath a dim streetlight with the engine running. The driver window was shot through, and pieces of glass lay in the dirt. A bloody figure sat behind the wheel—a young man from what I could see. Head back, eyes clocked wide.

Then I saw her—and it wasn't Mercy Dixon.

A woman with blood-soaked hair inched around the passenger side of the vehicle on her stomach, pulling her body forward with the palms of her hands. She looked up at me one-eyed and coughed out a word, but I couldn't understand. Half her face was pulpy and raw, like a can of dog food had exploded in her lap. It was a miracle she was moving at all. She left a wide swath of blood in the dirt behind her as she clawed and scraped toward me. Still, the words kept coming. I knelt down, and I could feel my booze-heavy heart chugging, the cool white air turning my arms to gooseflesh.

"My god," I said, then steeled myself. "I live nearby—I'm going to call for help."

It didn't seem to register.

Her gaze drifted over my shoulder.

"Be-hi . . . be-hind," she said.

A shadow passed over us, and her one good eye slipped up into the socket.

"Be-hind y-y-y," she said, and collapsed in the dirt.

I turned.

A large, stony-eyed man loomed over me. Late-thirties, thick brown mustache. He wore his hair very short in an army-style buzz cut, but the hairline sat high and receded into deep bald coves. His stomach drooped over the waist of his trousers and his shirttails hung untucked. He looked like a long-haul trucker who had jumped out of his rig in a hurry.

I could hear his breath, that big gut rising and falling.

In one hand, a glistening lead pipe dangled along the length of his thigh.

The other held a silver revolver.

"Turn around," he told me. "Don't look at me."

His tone was cordial, like it was just a friendly suggestion. Like someone giving directions to the beach, maybe. He raised the gun at me and thumbed the hammer back. He did it slowly, so I could hear every click. I tried turning around like he said, but my feet froze up on me. I thought the ratchet of that gun cylinder would be the last thing I ever heard.

"Go on," he said, smiling. "Just turn on back around."

***

I woke to a swirl of mechanical beeps and urgent voices chattering all around me. A doctor in white medical scrubs was shining a light into my eyes with his lips pursed, nodding and musing to himself.

"Are you with us, Mr. Kenney?" said the doctor. "Jack?"

I groaned.

My head hurt so bad a groan was all I could manage.

I blinked around the hospital room and saw it was full of cops. Six or seven maybe, all standing with their arms crossed over their blue uniforms. A sea of blond and brown mustaches. The doctor set his light down and turned to one of them.

"I'll give you five minutes with him," said the doctor. "Then I'll need to do some tests."

The doctor went away, and a silver-haired cop took his place.

"You know who I am, son?"

I shook my head the best I could.

"I'm the Chief of Police," he said. "Me and my boys are here to arrest you for the murders of . . ." he rattled off seven or eight names, some of which I recognized from the newspapers. The name Janice Balco stood out—the poet who wrote about whales. All the faces in the room watched me ghoulishly as the Chief finished his litany of the dead.

By now, the hospital lights had felt much too bright for my headache, and I raised my hand to shield my eyes—but my hands were cuffed to the sides of the bed.

"Once the doctor clears you, we'll bring you to the jail for booking," said the Chief. "The thrill kills stop here, fucko. I'm going to make sure you never see the light of day again."

A part of me thought it was a nightmare. With any luck, I was still passed out on the wharf with a half-eaten fish sandwich in my lap as the fog swirled around me and the sea lions barked in the cold black water.

"You got it wrong," I managed. *I saw him.*

"You saw who?"

"The killer." I tried to block the light again, and again my shackled wrists clattered against the hospital bed. "Big guy with a mustache and a buzz cut."

"That right?" said the Chief. He looked amused, gesturing around the room with his pudgy hands. "We're all big guys with mustaches. But you know what? Nobody found us unconscious with the murder weapon in our hands and our pockets full of thirty-eight caliber casings."

The Chief clucked and crowed until the doctor returned, and then the cops filed out into the hallway, throwing hateful looks over their shoulders as they went. When the doctor looked me over, I managed to give a slight tug on his coat.

"The killer knocked me out," I said. "Hit me hard on the back of the head. You see the wound—*you believe me, don't you?*"

The doctor shushed me and patted my chest.

"My daughter went to school with one of your victims, you sick son of a bitch," he said. "I hope you rot in hell."

***

My court-appointed attorney was with me when they brought me in for booking the next day, but neither of us made it through the crowd without getting drenched in spit and cold coffee. The whole town showed up to tell me exactly what they thought of me. I was still unsteady on my feet, and by the time I was fingerprinted and photographed, all I could do was sit in the booking area with my head between my knees.

A few hours later, I was alone in a concrete room with my lawyer, a gangly man with a bad hairpiece and a midwestern accent named Stan Jennings. He said the police wanted to get an official statement, and we only had a few minutes to talk. I asked him how they could mistake me for the killer when I was struck over the head from behind.

"They're going to say you slipped on the railroad tracks when you shot the girl," said Jennings. He said it matter-of-factly, like it had already been explained to him. "The doctor confirmed on record that your head injury is consistent with a fall. But it's a small matter compared to the preponderance of evidence against you."

"I didn't do it, Jennings," I said. I was heading into a full-blown panic—it felt like everyone had made up their minds while I was unconscious. "Whose side are you on, here?"

"I'm here to represent you, but I'm also an officer of the court."

"Then you should find the real killer—the man who hit me and planted the gun."

Jennings watched me with his fingers laced neatly on the table.

"You'll be treated fairly. I'll make sure of it. But the murder weapon is only one piece of it—an incriminating piece, to be sure—but only a piece. They're going to demonstrate how you were near the first murder scene when you left the bar on June 25th. They'll say how you finished your shift at the cement plant around the time of the Waddell Creek murders, just a few miles away. They found you at the latest crime scene, for god's sake. You had the opportunity to commit all three crimes, and yes, you were in possession of a .38 revolver and a pocketful of casings. You'll be treated fairly, I promise you that. But you're almost certainly going to prison for the rest of your life."

***

The District Attorney pursued the charges with great vigor.

They wanted to make a spectacle, and I was the man they had.

Things moved fast after the initial interrogation. The D.A. was determined to smother me in charges. By the time of the arraignment, I faced over sixty counts, and even though the state's death penalty laws were in flux, the D.A. swore he'd find a way to end my life any way he could—even if he had to do it with his bare hands.

Talk about a spectacle.

They kept me isolated from the rest of the jail population for my own safety, which I didn't mind at all. I showered and ate alone. The irony wasn't lost on me—they were keeping me alive long enough to kill me. Some nights, I felt like beating them to the punch. I felt lost and hopeless. My chickenshit attorney wanted me to plead guilty in exchange for *life without parole,* instead of coming up with any real legal strategy.

Then, two things happened that really changed the game.

The first happened to a kid named Victor Lara about two weeks into my incarceration. He was calling his mother from a payphone outside of the 7-Eleven on Laurel Street when someone in a white pickup pulled to the curb and shot him five times with a .45 caliber pistol. The gun was different, and the one-on-one nature of the crime didn't fit the pattern, but it was enough to cause a lot of handwringing. The fact that Lara's mother heard the whole thing over the phone made for a juicy front-page article. There was even a witness who said the driver had snapped a photograph before speeding off but couldn't give a description. Even Jennings grew a backbone and wanted to talk strategy. At the very least, he thought the D.A. might come back with a better deal.

Then, three days after Victor Lara's murder, the COs shackled me and brought me into a quiet meeting room and sat me in the corner. They ran a chain from my wrists to an eyelet on the floor so I couldn't stand. A few minutes later, Jennings entered—followed by a woman with eyeglasses and a gray ponytail.

"I didn't think I was allowed visitors," I said.

Sandra Dixon entered the room tentatively, hands raised to her mouth as if stifling a cry.

"I'm so sorry," she blurted. "We all thought—they were so sure. Your name was all over the papers."

I looked at Jennings, who now wore a bland smile.

"There's been a development," he said. He showed me a book of poems by Emily Dickinson. "You read much poetry?"

"I'll read every damn word if it gets me out of here."

"You won't have to," said Jennings. He never looked me in the eye but today was different. He turned to Sandra and handed her a handkerchief. "You said you wanted to tell him yourself?"

Sandra wiped her eyes and nodded.

"Mercy saw what happened. She must have been wandering the neighborhood that night, looking for the moon. I'm so sorry it took this long to find it, hiding in plain sight."

"Find what?"

"Her journal entry from the night you—well, the night you were attacked."

Sandra handed me a leather journal embossed with all the moon cycles and told me to find the entry for July 28th. I had trouble finding it, so she flipped the pages, ran her finger down the text, and read the entry over my shoulder.

All the Heavens were a Cloud,
A Night of pungent Tides,
When came a Scream like shrieking Gulls,
Beneath the Lamppost's shine.
And when the Fog scattered through—
A Man with shaven Head,
And ample Flesh upon his Waist
Swung down his Club of Lead.

I read it three or four times.

"My god. Mercy wrote this?"

The pair nodded.

"Will it make a difference?"

"It very well could be enough." He folded his arms and gave a slow nod, talking it through. "It's not a perfect witness testimony, and we'll need to see if Mercy can give us more, but it corroborates your statement perfectly. And the date's right. I've gone through all of Dickinson's published poems and can't find a match. It's derivative, but it's Mercy's own words. If you add the Lara murder into the mix, we have our reasonable doubt. The killer's still out there. I give it even odds they drop all charges."

I handed the diary back to Sandra.

"I promised you I'd look out for her, but she was the one looking out for me."

Sandra put a hand on my shoulder.

"We're looking out for each other, like you said."

***

It took the D.A. another three weeks to do the right thing.

It was a long three weeks.

One of the COs let a local kid named Jimmy Cardinale break my nose when I was coming out of the shower. It bled for two days straight. And I could never get over the suspicion they were messing with my food somehow. My stomach hurt every night after dinner, and someone banged on my cell door at all hours so I couldn't get any sleep.

But none of that mattered the day I walked out.

Jennings gave me a bottle of bourbon and a ride to the municipal wharf, where I bought a fish sandwich and watched the fog roll in over the bay. I must have looked like a maniac sitting there, medical tape over the bridge of my nose and two sooty black eyes, falling into a cottony web of inebriation. I kept that routine for a month straight, talking to no one, keeping to myself. No one seemed to recognize me. Occasionally, the cops would check me out, but they gave me a wide berth as if I were cursed—*the only person to face the Seaside Stalker and live to tell the tale.* I still had my apartment, but I'd been fired from my jobs. I didn't care about any of that, as long as I was free.

The chief resigned soon after, and the D.A. lost his reelection bid in the fall.

Then, on Christmas Day, a large man with a buzz cut and a binder full of grisly Polaroid photos walked into the police station and turned himself in. Rodney Langaniere was a local cab driver for Speedy Cab, and by his own account, he was in the murder business purely for sport. He collected the photos like baseball cards, all neatly tucked into plastic protective sheets. He'd been at it longer than anyone thought, and they connected him to eighteen murders up and down the coast. Langaniere said his victims spoke to him through the Polaroids, and when the whispers grew unbearable, he figured it was time to hang up his hat.

I started bartending again, and soon enough, they rehired me at the cement plant. Things returned to normal, as they often do, and when I got back on my feet, I bought a telescope at the new Sears department store. A nice one from Edmund Scientific with big eight-inch reflectors that let you see the rings of Saturn and all the moons. On clear nights, I'd carry it to Sandra Dixon's place under my arm and set it up in the backyard so Mercy could see the moon as big as her face, with all the shadowy craters and everything. Eventually, I let her keep it. She'd study the heavens until her eyes got red and watery, turning the knobs with those spidery white fingers. Then she'd journal about what she'd seen in verse form, and they were lovely little poems.

The Block and the Chain

They meet at the Plumed Horse in Saratoga, a Michelin Star restaurant with tableside duck consommé and the kind of desserts that float by on elegant glass-domed carts. He's relieved when she walks through the door—in these days of deep fakes and filters, it's hard to know if a *TikTok ten* will translate to an *IRL ten*, and from what he can tell, everything checks out. He lets her wait at the hostess stand for a moment, watching as she scans the room. He doesn't want to seem eager. When he finally stands and waives her over, he adjusts the cuff of his sleeve so everyone can see the rose-gold Bulova on his wrist.

"Brooks?" she says, with cautious eyes.

He knows it's an act—based on her profile, there's nothing cautious about her.

"Cecilia? Please, sit. I ordered you a Malvasia Bianca."

She hangs her clutch on the chair and settles into the immaculate white-cloth two-top. She slowly drags a long strand of brown hair behind her ear and smiles broadly—it's enough to trigger her dimples. Brooks knows this must be a signature move, and he's surprised she's played it so early. Still, he gives her the reaction she's looking for and offers a smile in return.

He wants to reward her for acting pretty and insecure.

"Sorry I'm late," she says.

"It's only a minute or two."

His eyes drift over her dress.

"I didn't recognize the flag on your profile," he says.

"Panamá," she says. "I'm from Panama City. You been there?" She plays up the long vowels in the word *city*. She thinks he has an accent kink, and she's not wrong. Brooks won't date a woman unless he knows English is her second language. He thinks it gives him an advantage—and power is an aphrodisiac.

"I've never been," he says. "But if you're any indication, I'll have to change that."

"That's very nice of you."

It's the most reassurance he'll give until dinner ends.

From now on, everything will be about him.

"It's called the blockchain," he says later, when the wine comes. He rolls a glass of Mourvèdre in the air and waits for her to admit she doesn't know what that is. "It's a digital ledger—a way to do business without gatekeepers like banks or federal governments. It's okay—not many people understand it. But that's how I make a living. It's like being involved with the Internet in '89 or computing in the 1940s. I'm one of the early adopters. There are exchanges for cryptocurrencies and I help clients navigate them. It's all very lucrative for me."

"Is it like Bitcoin?" she asks.

This time he doesn't reward her with a smile.

"That's one of many digital currencies, but you're on the right track."

"I should introduce you to my tío, Inácio," she says. "He's always looking for new ways to move money around." But she covers her mouth after she says it, and her eyes track left and right to see if anyone is listening.

"Your uncle's a businessman?"

"Yes." She lowers her voice. "He lives in Panamá, but he visits the Bay Area all the time. He's in town this week for something called vulture capital."

"You mean *venture capital?*"

"Yes, that's it. I'll give him your number if it's okay with you."

Brooks worries the power dynamic has shifted now that she has something to offer beyond what's under her dress.

"I might have room for one more client," he says. "No guarantees, though."

***

It bothers him that Cecilia doesn't fawn over his high-end loft on Santa Cruz Avenue. She's the first of his dates to see it after the remodel—the exposed brick and concrete countertops. The NFT nudes framed over the bed. He worries that she's seen better lofts in other parts of town. When he undresses her, he makes sure to toss her clothes all over the room so he can lay in bed and watch her search for them afterward. He sometimes wonders if this is another one of his kinks or just a personality disorder.

Later, when the rideshare comes, he walks her down to the lamp-lit street and they hug like friends and kiss on the cheek. They don't make plans to see each other again—that's another dance that must be carefully choreographed—but as he's riding the small elevator back to his loft, his phone rings and he assumes she's forgotten something.

He answers—it's a voice he doesn't recognize.

"I understand you are the crypto guy," says the voice, a hoarse, accented croak that triggers the hair on his forearms.

"I'm sorry, who am I speaking with?"

"My name is Inácio Narra. My niece sent me your number tonight, says you're the *real deal*."

"Of course—*Cecilia,*" says Brooks. He clears his throat and turns his crypto-bro vibe up to maximum sleaze. "She spoke highly of you and your business. She said we should meet."

"Yes, I agree. Don't you? How about tonight?"

The phosphorescent hands of the Bulova read one in the morning.

"We must be in different time zones," says Brooks.

"I can assure you we are in the same time zone, amigo. Here's what I propose. Meet me at your office in thirty minutes to discuss opening a new account with your firm. My driver already has the address. For your trouble, we will only consider seven-digit wire transfers. Do we have a deal?"

Brooks enters the loft and fingers the blinds as if he might find Mr. Narra in a tinted sedan idling on the street, watching him.

"Yeah sure," says Brooks. He doesn't like to be summoned, but he also senses a tinge of urgency, and it excites something in his cells. "Let's do it."

***

When Brooks reaches his boutique streetside office in Los Gatos, all the lights are on and there's a Mercedes idling at the curb. The door is unlocked. There's a sharp smell of cologne inside, something like tobacco and eucalyptus. A large man blocks the doorway of his personal office and Brooks knows this cannot be Mr. Narra. The vibe is wrong: he's too young and his eyes are dull and flat like someone is controlling him from a distance. The large man beckons Brooks forward and pats him down from pits to ankles.

"No need for that, Santos," says a voice—*Narra's voice*. It's coming from deeper in the office. "We are all professional businessmen here."

The large man steps aside, and Brooks sees Mr. Narra seated at his desk with his feet up. He's a petite man with a neatly trimmed beard that has turned mostly gray, save for a darker patch on his chin. Silver curls hang at his ears and forehead, black chevrons for eyebrows. He has the kind of lines on his face that make him both handsome and fearsome at the same time.

"If you're wondering how we got in," says Mr. Narra, "it would be easier to just skip that part and get straight to business."

Brooks considers his personal office a spider web for wealthy clients. A sticky trap for easy five-figure commissions. But now there was a new spider plucking the threads—*the kind that eats other spiders.*

"Normally my clients like to talk about the blockchain and all the emerging crypto currencies available to them," says Brooks. He squeezes into one of the chairs he reserves for his clients—too small by design—and folds his hands awkwardly in his lap. "It's an exciting opportunity, but it's also an evolving landscape and you should—"

"Can you tell me about chain-hopping?" says Narra. He leans forward and now his blue-gray eyes have a sinister interest that almost looks like hunger.

"Sure, I mean you just convert digital currencies through a series of different exchanges to achieve greater—"

"Do you know of any rules against it?"

Brooks turns up his palms like he's about to fill the room with insight.

"In my business you learn there are two sets of rules, Mr. Narra. There is a set of rules for the regular nine-to-five chump who thinks it's a civic duty to let everyone shove taxes and bank fees and interest charges straight up his colon. And there are rules for smart men who routinely get *ten-X* on their investments through pure ingenuity and creative financial management. My guess is you are one of the latter, am I right? If so, I'm not so much concerned about the rules, and you shouldn't be either. We can usually work around them."

Mr. Narra nods approvingly.

Brooks knows it's the answer he was hoping for.

"In that case," says Mr. Narra. "I would like to open an account. How long would it take to chain-hop five million dollars?"

Brooks feels sweat trailing down the back of his neck. He hopes Mr. Narra doesn't notice, but with those eager, hungry eyes how could he not?

"We'll do a little paperwork and I'll send you the account numbers in the morning. You can begin the wire transfers whenever you'd like," says Brooks. "When the money lands, I'll make you my top priority. How does that sound?"

Mr. Narra signals to Santos, who unshoulders a black gym bag and sets it atop the desk. Brooks knows without unzipping it that it's full of dirty cash. He can see the hard corners pressing through the nylon. *It excites him.*

"I like to pay my commissions separately. I don't like when the account balances shrink without explanation, okay? It's six percent, but it's all cash—so you can do whatever you want with it. Live your best life. I've got more nieces to fuck if you're interested."

"I understand—yes. I can do that."

"Good. And one more thing, amigo. When I call you, I expect you to answer. No text, no voicemail. I don't care if you're in a meeting or at the dentist or getting the best blowjob of your life. You answer. Every fucking time—you answer. *Understand?*"

"Yes. I understand."

***

The first sign of trouble comes on a rainy morning in November.

Brooks's phone goes *ding ding ding* as he turns the corner onto University Avenue, an umbrella in one hand and a 190-degree venti caramel Macchiato—*hold the foam and the tip*—in the other. He doesn't check the texts until his assistant, Kimberly, greets him at the door with a wild look and the sound of landlines at DEFCON ONE.

"Did you hear?" she says, with a TV remote in her hand.

He sets the umbrella behind the door, glances at the phone on her desk.

All the lights are blinking red.

"Hear what?"

She swings the remote at the TV, jerking the volume button as if it would somehow work faster that way. Brooks sees a pretty TV anchor with glossy lips and a robot stare. She's talking about one of the main crypto exchanges Brooks uses, and how the company that runs it has filed for bankruptcy. There's even a photograph of the company's CEO, a young tech bro named Zander Holman-Reid, with the caption: POSSIBLE INDICTMENT?

The anchor repeats the words *liquidity* and *loss* and *shockwaves*.

Brooks's cell phone rings in his hand.

It's Mr. Narra.

FUCK.

Brooks answers—at least he thinks he answers. The words stick to his tongue like bad medicine.

"Sounds like my crypto wizard is having quite the day," says Narra. "Hopefully it doesn't mean I'm having one, too."

"I'm about to make some phone calls," says Brooks. "I'm sure it's not as bad as it sounds."

"You better be sure." Narra's mouth is close to the phone and Brooks can hear the topography of his throat as he speaks. The tiny balls of phlegm, the tobacco-scarred bronchial tubes. Maybe he's smoking a cigarette, maybe he's already smoked too many. "Because it sounds very bad to me. How much of my account has been anonymized?"

"About half."

"And how much of that is liquid?"

"Also half."

"Well, that's not so good. You might have to go to extraordinary lengths to make me whole. I trust that I am still your top priority?"

Brooks has visions of his tongue slowly pulled through a slit in his throat to make a Colombian necktie. *Is Panama near Colombia?*

"Yes, of course you are my top priority."

"Good, amigo. That's very good."

***

The day feels like a week.

By the end of the week—*eons.*

Clients line up at his office to dress him down. They call him a fraud and a liar. He hears comparisons to Bernie Madoff.

He doesn't really care about name-calling, but the legal threats worry him. Everything is beyond his control, and he can't help any of it—it's like someone emptied a tube of crazy glue into the crypto market.

Amid the media circus and the unending drop-ins, Brooks breaks the one promise he swore to keep. It happens while a client named Van Hoevel is standing in his office, telling him about a bulldog lawyer who will *turn him inside out*. Brooks doesn't know what that means exactly, but during the litany of threats and oaths, he lets a call from Mr. Narra go unanswered.

When he sees the notification, a rotten feeling grows.

He waits until later that night, a bottle of twenty-year Macallan at the ready. He plays Narra's message, and the first time through, he's relieved—there's no yelling or swearing, nothing spoken at all. All he hears is the slow rasp of Narra's breath, like it's an old school answering machine and he's waiting for Brooks to pick up. The message breaks apart into white noise with each slow breath. It's like that for fifteen seconds—then there's a sparkwheel of a cigarette lighter, the crackle of tobacco, a long drag, and the message ends.

He replays it again and feels unsettled.

By the tenth time through—he's terrified.

***

He's drunk when he calls Cecilia.

She doesn't pick up, so he calls again.

And again.

When she finally answers, it sounds like she's at a party. A bass track thrums in the background like a heartbeat on crank. She shouts into the phone—partly because of the loud music, partly because she's annoyed.

"It's about your uncle," he says.

"I already gave him your number." She says it fast like she's trying to end the call in a hurry.

"I know—we're doing business together. I just need to talk to you."

"What do you want, Brooks?" There's a bite to her voice, as if she's close to hanging up on him. "We went on like *one date* and I never heard from you again. Get to the point."

"I fucked up with him. I think he's really upset with me."

"That's your problem. Leave me out of it."

"I'm not asking for help, here. I just need to know something about him."

There's a long pause and the music fades. It sounds like she's gone into a private room or stepped outside.

"He's family," she says. "I won't tell you much."

"I just need to know how dangerous he is. Like if he's upset with me, you know, would he try to hurt me? What's his deal, really?"

"If you've angered him, you'll want to make it up to him very quickly."

"Yeah, but what if I can't? I mean, what if he thinks I really screwed him over—like a *million-dollar-plus* screw-over? I'm kind of freaking out here."

A long pause, then: "Goodbye, Brooks. Don't call me again."

"*No no—wait!*"

The call ends.

He tries texting her, but all the messages go unread.

***

The news only gets worse.

Next day, he learns Zander Holman-Reid has fled to some Caribbean country with minimal extradition laws and a local court has issued an injunction against market-making on the exchange. It's a clumsy move—the courts don't know how to handle this. Panic begets more panic. The contagion spreads to other tech markets and there are worries it could bleed into the broader financial market. Trading is briefly halted on the NASDAQ.

There's a tight pain in Brooks's stomach like a fist clenching. He does a line of cocaine off the concrete countertop and texts Kimberly, tells her not to come in for the rest of the week. She asks if she'll still get paid, and he says no. Kimberly quits. It doesn't hurt his feelings—he didn't hire her for her clerical skills.

More cocaine.

The fist unclenches, but the paranoia grows.

Some steampunk-looking Derringer pistol comes out of the drawer, and he paces around the loft, wagging it at the walls, shouting obscenities at the TV.

He orders Grubhub from an overpriced American-style bistro in Saratoga. He won't touch French fries unless they're double-fried with garlic aioli. When the order comes, he tells the delivery guy to leave it at the door, but the guy doesn't listen, just keeps knocking.

They always leave it at the door—*don't they?*

Knock knock knock.

Brooks checks the doorbell camera. Some skinny kid with an Adam's apple like the knuckle of a big toe. He's wearing earbuds and bobbing his head to a mid-tempo beat. Brooks has done so much cocaine he can almost feel the beat clapping in his veins.

KNOCK KNOCK KNOCK.

"Just fucking leave it," he shouts.

KNOCK KNOCK KNOCK.

Brooks throws open the door, tears the bag out of the kid's hands, and screams *fuck you* in Neanderthal. The kid sees the gun and his eyes clock wide. He pedals back, holds up his hands, and bolts down the hall.

The fries are cold, but Brooks eats them anyway.

***

He's crying in the shower when they come for him.

Brooks sees them as he staggers out of the bathroom with a big white robe and bloodshot eyes. He freezes. They seem bored and disinterested, like they're waiting for a table at a restaurant. Like breaking into high-end lofts is part of their day-to-day.

"You look like a wet bag of cocaine," says Mr. Narra. He puffs on a cigarette and flicks the ashes onto the floor. Santos stands at his side, hands on his hips. His holstered pistol says *don't even fucking try.*

"I need more time," says Brooks.

A laugh—it sounds like a cat hissing.

"Time to do what? More drugs and alcohol?"

"I can get your money out."

"No, you can't. You don't think I've looked into this? Even if you could get the money out, the currency valuation has fallen through the floor. Beyond the floor, really—straight down into the devil's greasy asshole. Who knows if it will ever recover?"

"None of this is my fault. It just happened."

Mr. Narra doesn't like this.

"What a childish statement. *It just happened?*"

"Everyone's scrambling. Nobody knows what to do."

Mr. Narra gives a disgusted look and tilts his head to Santos, who unholsters a flat black pistol with a suppressor and levels it at Brooks.

"Adelante," says Santos, flicking the pistol at the door.

Brooks holds his hands up.

"Where are we going?"

Santos's eyes grow large and a growl burbles deep in his throat.

"Santos never repeats anything," says Mr. Narra. "If he does, it means your ass. I'd better move if I were you."

Brooks shuffles to the door, glancing around the loft to see where he left his Derringer. He doesn't see it anywhere. In the hallway, he considers making a run for it, but the halls are too long and Santos is too close. He feels the pistol in his spine, urging him onward toward the elevator. He thinks they're going down to the street, but they take the stairs instead—one flight up to the roof. Santos and Narra are wearing black masks and leather gloves—*were they wearing them the whole time?*

"I want to tell you a funny story," says Mr. Narra, amid the woosh and whir of rooftop ventilation units. It's late evening and there's a spectacular Central Coast sunset playing out over the Santa Cruz Mountains, redwoods serrating a dark orange sky. To the east, evening commuters claw their way home along Highway 17 toward Santa Cruz, headlights winding through the gloom like a string of patio lights. "When I was a young man, I worked for my father. I kept an eye on things, made sure everyone did their jobs. Mid-management, but for the transshipment business. Mostly moving Colombian cocaine through the canal. I'm sure none of this surprises you. Most of the time, it was an easy job. But when someone betrayed our trust, there was this thing we'd do. I'd arrange for the Port Authority to take us out into the canal—we had plenty of PA guys in our pockets—and then we'd wrap the guy in a heavy steel chain and loop it through a few concrete cinder blocks and sink him in the canal. You have to make an example of somebody now and then to keep order, as I'm sure you can imagine." Here comes that sinister, feline laugh again. "So when I first heard the term *blockchain*, that's what I imagined. I can't untangle the two concepts. I must have sunk a dozen men in that canal. All tied up in blockchains—*cadenas de bloques.*"

They're standing at the edge of the building. A three-foot-tall barrier encircles the rooftop, and Brooks sees a small step stool pressed against the rail. Beside the stepstool is a heavy steel chain coiled in a mound, and there's a concrete cinder block resting beside it.

Brooks knows he's going to die.

He makes one last attempt to flee—he spins around Santos and runs toward the stairwell door. Santos is quick—he brings the pistol down on Brooks's head and opens a two-inch gash in his scalp. Brooks goes down, blood spilling over his white terrycloth robe. Santos stands him up again.

The world blurs.

"Please," says Brooks. He says it to the fuzzy masked figures before him. He says it to the universe. He knows that begging is his only play now. "I learned my lesson. I'll do better. I'll make it right."

"It isn't you who needs a lesson," says Mr. Narra. "You are beyond instruction. We considered killing you with that stupid cartoon gun we found in your apartment to make it look like a suicide. Thing is, it's my other financial partners who really need to learn from this. The financial landscape is evolving, as you recently told me. My people need to be reminded where they stand."

Brooks only hears half of it. The rest is drowned by the sound of chains coiling around his neck. Santos places the cinder block atop the ledge. The chain is wrapped through its hollow center to make a crude anchor.

"De rodillas," says Santos.

Brooks doesn't know what this means.

He blinks at the city lights. There are pigeons flying low over the cityscape, returning to their night roosts. The fang of a crescent moon rises out of the South Bay smog.

The cinder block vanishes.

In its place: the chain snakes wildly against the ledge.

It makes a sound like spare coins emptying from a glass jug.
The slack runs out and the chain snaps tight.
The world spins and wrenches apart.

Whatever Kills the Pain

September, 1960

"Could somebody please turn up the television?" said Ma, from her deathbed.

Claire had helped her sit upright with a nest of pillows behind her neck and back, and now there were so many pillows it was a wonder she could see over them all. She was wearing Pa's old seeing glasses and it made her eyes look big and spider-like with the lashes pressed up against the lenses.

"Where are they?" said Ma. "In a Hollywood studio?"

"They're in Chicago," said Claire. "They announced it a minute ago."

"Well, if it's a beauty contest, my vote's for Kennedy. Nixon looks like he's got one foot in the grave. Just look at him, the poor thing. Rode hard and put away wet."

Joe lumbered into the room with blackberry jam on his cheeks, his boots muddy and untied.

"Kennedy is going to space," he said.

"He's not going to space," said Claire, studying the television with her arms crossed. It was a hand-me-down from the Comstocks when they upgraded to an RCA color TV last summer, and it was a much nicer model than they could have afforded on their own. Claire suspected they'd passed it down simply because they didn't want to bother hauling it away—it wasn't like them to be so kind. "Space is too dangerous for politicians. That's what astronauts are for."

"He's going to space," Joe insisted, but now he wore a mischievous grin, blackberry seeds burrowed deep into the pickets of his teeth. "Kennedy's an astronaut, but it's a secret. He's gonna sneak onto a rocketship and *blast off.*"

"Yeah, and Ma's a secret astronaut, too," said Claire. "And maybe so are you, Joey. When are you gonna *blast off?*" She poked his belly and he giggled wildly, guarding his body with jam-covered hands.

"Don't, Sissy," he said, squealing. "You stop it right now."

"Is that a cut on your hand, or blackberry jam?"

"It's not a cut. It's jam, that's all it is."

Ma groaned and batted a skeletal hand in the air.

"I can't hear a damn thing," she said. "Pipe down or get out."

They made it halfway through the programming before Ma's breathing labored and it became impossible to focus on the debate. There was talk of the economy, education, the Soviet Union—but what Claire wanted to know was how long the pain medicine would last before Ma's cancer tore her to pieces. Nobody had a ready-made answer for this, nor did she expect one. Still, the new decade had brought with it a sense of optimism, and she hoped, at minimum, to hear what new direction the country would go and what her place would be in it.

"Go to your room for a minute or two," Claire said to Joe. "Play with your rocket ships while I help Ma with her medicine."

Joe was about to protest, but Ma gave another deathly groan. Her eyes rolled back, and a tremor started up her body, knuckles rapping against the headboard. She peered across the room as if everyone had suddenly vanished, skin taut against her cheekbones like an old leather chair, then she settled into the pillows, panting.

"She's getting sicker," said Joe, with the earnestness of a judge. He backed slowly out of the room, boots clomping one after the other. "The medicine's not working."

"I told you—it's pain medicine, Joey," said Claire. "That's all it's for."

When Joe left the room, Claire set Ma upright and poured the liquid morphine into a small wooden spoon and carefully served it to her. Sometimes Ma would choke and the medicine would come trailing out the corners of her mouth and Claire would have to scrape it off her chin before it dripped into the bedding. This time, it went down without any trouble. Soon, Ma's breathing steadied and her slow eyes found Claire at the end of the bed.

"Who won?" said Ma.

"What?"

"The debate. Who won the debate?"

"They didn't announce a winner," said Claire. "I suppose it depends on who you ask."

Ma was quiet for a moment, her breath slow and even like a sleeper.

"Is it funny that I care about it, even if I'm not long for the world?" said Ma, almost whispering. "Just because my life is fading away doesn't mean yours is. I'll still be your mother, even when my soul thunders up to the Heavens. I'll still want things to be better for you and Joey down here on Earth."

Claire wiped her eyes with her fingertips. "I know you will, Ma."

"Good. Now be a good girl and fetch your father's revolver from the closet."

"Ma?"

"Don't worry. I just want to see it is all."

"It's still there, last I checked."

"Just bring it on down, would you?"

Claire rose and found the blue milkcrate in the corner of the room and walked it to the closet. She climbed up so she could reach the cigar box on the top shelf. A silverfish skittered over her hand and she flicked it against the wall with her fingernail. She flipped the lid and found the blue velveteen bag where Pa had kept his old Smith and Wesson, then returned to the edge of the bed with the bag cinched tight, as if opening it would fill the room with bees.

"Show it to me, will you?" said Ma, with a soft and faraway voice.

Claire loosened the draw and slipped the gun out. Heavy and cold. It smelled like shop grease. She held it in the shallows of her palms and turned to Ma as one might offer water to a thirsty animal.

Ma's old eyes fixed on the gun knowingly.

"It gives me peace of mind, you know," she said. "In case the medicine runs out."

***

In the morning, they gathered tools from the backyard shed and trundled up the weedy two-track to the Comstock house. The house was a three-story Victorian from the timber boom era that sat above a terraced vineyard. Much of the lumber used for the construction had been milled from redwood on the property, and the forest loomed from all directions as if wanting to reclaim the land it once occupied. Claire couldn't remember a time they hadn't lived in the little groundsman quarters at the bottom of the hill. One of her earliest memories was her brother Joe coming into the world in the same room their mother was about to exit.

It was Monday, and on Mondays they began by picking small branches and pinecones from the front and back lawns before running the lawnmower they stored in a shed nearby. Joe had pleaded for years to operate the lawnmower, and it wasn't until his sixteenth birthday that Claire finally relented. Eight months later, he still mowed with a self-satisfied grin, eyes proud, as if he were piloting an airplane through a dangerous storm. Claire raked around the carefully manicured hedges and trimmed any errant sprouts that she could find. As she worked toward the front of the house, she found a redwood branch that had fallen against the building and shattered a low basement window. She cleared the branch and dragged it across the lawn to the treeline, Joe slowing his march to watch her.

"That's a big branch, Sissy," he shouted over the roar of the mower.

Claire gave a thumbs up. "Big enough to break a window."

"What?"

"A window," she said, pointing. "It broke a basement window."

Joe idled the mower and looked where she was pointing.

"Oh darn it all," he said, a phrase he'd learned from Ma. "Poor little window."

Claire found a pair of thick leather gloves in the gardening bucket and collected the shards from the sill. She figured once she'd cleaned up the glass, she could nail a board over the opening until it could be repaired properly. A larger shard had fallen inside, resting on top of a bookcase, and as she reached for it, she noticed the basement was in a state of disarray, shelves toppled and boxes torn and emptied. She scooted back to get a better look and her foot knocked something heavy beneath the hedges. She fished it out and turned it over in her hands—a sterling silver candlestick. There were more items scattered here—a silver fork, a fine China plate with a grapevine relief stamped into the center.

"Joey," said Claire. He was standing with the mower sputtering, watching her from across the lawn. "Turn that off and go grab a couple burlap sacks from the shed. You know where to find them."

He killed the motor and pointed at the candlestick.

"What is that, Sissy?"

"It belongs to the Comstocks," she said. "I think there was a break-in. Go get those sacks so we can collect it all, why don't you?"

"A break-in? *Oh darn it all.*" He said it again and again with his hands atop his head, stomping across the fresh-cut lawn toward the lower property. *"Darn it, darn it."*

Claire circled the house, sweeping her foot under the hedges, looking for more items that may have been dropped. She'd heard of burglaries closer to town, but never this far into the country. Sometimes the Comstocks hired men from town to tend the vineyards or make small repairs to the house, but she hadn't seen or heard anyone coming up the narrow dirt road in several days. Weeks, even.

She was returning to the broken window with more items cradled in her arms when she found Bill Comstock standing in the yard, watching her. He wore a dress shirt and slacks with a striped red tie, the stub of a lit cigar pinched between his fingers. The way his hair lay slicked and wet-looking gave him a patina of mob-like connectedness.

"Whatcha got there, sweetheart?" he said, with a lukewarm grin.

Claire laid everything in the grass and waved her arms over it as if she were still trying to make sense of what happened.

"I think there was a break-in," she said, feeling the unexpected weight of suspicion. She'd always felt Bill was cold to her, even when they were little. He would peer from his third-story bedroom with the drapes parted as she tended the yard with her Pa, like some bored prison guard watching an inmate, yearning for a chance to shoot. He was the youngest of the Comstock brothers, closest in age to Claire, and she often wondered if that was what made the dynamic so wrought. "They broke a basement window with a redwood branch, and I found all this scattered around. At first I thought it was the wind, but—" She gestured at the collection at her feet again. "We can board it up for you. The broken window, that is."

He gave his cigar a noisy puff before sending it pinwheeling across the lawn.

"My mother always thought you were stealing from us," he said. "Whenever something would go missing in the house, she'd say *oh, I bet it was those squatters down the road.*"

"Oh no, Mr. Comstock," she said. "We've never stolen a thing."

"It's okay to call me Bill."

"We've never taken from you, Bill. I've never even been inside the house."

"But that's not true, is it? I remember when you came over for a birthday party. I don't know whose idea it was to invite you—not mine. Was I six? Seven? You ate so many cupcakes they had to run to the kitchen and bake more. Like it was the first time you'd ever tasted chocolate. Or maybe you were stashing them away for your dimwitted brother? Tell me you don't remember."

"Yes, I remember," said Claire. "That was a long time ago."

"But you said *never.* That was a lie."

"Not a lie. Just misremembered."

"Misremembered? That's a fancy word for a girl like you." He stepped closer and slipped his hands in his pockets. "So who are you for, anyway? Nixon or Kennedy?"

She repeated his question, stalling for time, trying to figure a way out of the conversation. The way he said it, she knew he expected a particular answer.

"We're not following the election."

"Bullshit. Everyone's following the election. Tell you what. My brother and I are going to a Nixon rally down in Monterey next weekend. We're cutting him a check, so we'll get to shake his hand and everything." He studied her to see whether his words had sparked any interest. They hadn't. "Come with us and listen to what he has to say. There's still time to 'Click with Dick'."

"Oh, I couldn't leave. Ma's sick and Joe needs looking after."

He leaned closer still, murmuring in her ear.

"I wonder what the Sheriff's Office would say if I told them my whole life, we've suspected you were stealing from us, and then I finally caught you red-handed? Would they believe it was *just the wind*, as you said?"

"All you caught me doing was recovering what someone left behind."

She took a step back and he matched it with a step closer.

"Now you're contradicting me."

"I work for you, Mr. Comstock. *Bill*. I would never—"

"There's that word again," he said, eyes darting around the property as if making sure they were alone. *"Never, never, never."* She smelled the musty cigar smoke on his clothes, the pomade. He took a length of her hair and combed his fingers through it. That unkind grin again, barely showing teeth. "You poor thing. I have so much power over you, and you don't even know it."

"Please, I—"

Claire tried to back away, but he'd tightened his grip on her hair, wound it up in his fist like a tether. She cried out as he drove her to the ground, holding her face in the grass. She took him by the wrist and tried to build slack so she could look him in the eyes and tell him to stop, but he was too strong. All she could do was plead.

"Please. Oh my god, please stop."

Then she heard Joe's voice and felt a different kind of fear. She couldn't see him, but she could hear him stomping over the lawn, calling her name. It sounded like he was starting up the lawnmower again. "Just go Joey, *run back home!*"

Bill turned to see who was coming, and whatever caught him in the face almost hit Claire, too. Bill fell away and the lawnmower crashed down beside her, the mower blade breaking free and spinning loose on the ground.

Claire got to her feet—she was afraid to look at what Joe had done, afraid to think about what consequences might come—but she looked anyway. Bill lay on his back, eyes skittering like a man trapped underwater. The lawnmower blade had nearly cleaved his face in two. His jaw had unhinged from the joint on the left side, and from his ruined mouth a bloody tongue lolled, torn from its fleshy cage.

She spoke calmly to Joe, who was now whimpering, hands on top of his head.

"Don't look at him," she said, but he kept looking anyway. "Don't you dare look at him, okay? You're not allowed to look."

Joe's eyes found Claire and steadied.

"He was—he was—"

"I know, Joey. You were only helping me."

"Yeah," he said, tears streaming down. "Just—just helping Sissy."

The sputtering grew more urgent, and she briefly lost Joe's attention to it. It sounded like he was choking on his own blood. He wormed in the grass with his hands at his throat, boot heels carving furrows into the grass.

Her mind worked quickly, picking through all the permutations of what could be done and at what cost.

"Look at me, Joe. Not him. The more you look, the less likely you'll ever forget it. You helped me and now you're my big hero, okay? But I need you to do something really important now. It's really, really important."

"Okay," he said, sobbing. "W-what is it?"

"I need you to run and get the wheelbarrow. Can you do that for me?"

"Yes, I can do it."

Bill's choking trailed off, then fell to silence. His boots stopped kicking. The abrupt end to the man's struggle made them both want to look, but Claire took Joe's tear-streaked face in her hands and kept him centered.

"Good. Don't get distracted. Come straight back. Run. Got it?"

"Got it."

***

She hooded Bill Comstock's slick and disfigured head with a burlap sack and pulled the rough fiber drawstring as if preparing him for a firing squad. By the stillness of the body and the pond of blood in the grass, Claire knew it was more of a funeral shroud. When Joe reappeared at the edge of the lawn, he was steering the old rusty wheelbarrow, and his pants were brindled with mud as if he'd fallen more than once along the way. They loaded the body, and Claire took hold of the long oak handles.

"Are we taking him to a doctor?" said Joe.

"No. A doctor couldn't help him anyway."

"Maybe they can give him stitches."

"He would need more than stitches, Joey Bear." She took up the handles and started toward the rock road with the little rubber wheel jittering under the weight. It took all her effort to stay calm and not panic Joe—all while imagining what they'd do to him if they found out. "Besides, we'd be in a lot of trouble if anyone learns about this. It has to be a secret, okay? A family secret that only you and I can know."

"What about Ma?"

"I'll tell her. I don't want you talking to her about it."

"Because she'll be mad at me?"

"Mad isn't the right word."

"She'll be mad 'cause I mowed on his face?"

She glanced at Bill's body, the blood now darkening through the burlap. They were halfway to the house on the lower property, and she was searching for the narrow coyote trail that led out into the redwoods to a secret place only the two of them knew about. A place Joe was forbidden to visit alone.

"Maybe she'd be a little mad," said Claire, kicking at the tanoak scrub. "That's why you need to let me handle it, okay?"

"Okay."

"I just need your help with one more thing."

Joe gave a ponderous look, like he wanted to guess.

"Are we going to the *Bunny Cave?*"

"Yes," she said, heaving the grisly load onto the trail. "Very good guess."

She wondered what could have been said for things to turn out differently, what she might have told Bill to calm things down. Some lie or ruse—a half truth, maybe. Or would Bill have attacked her no matter what? She imagined him waiting at his childhood window for a chance to see her alone, plotting some wicked fantasy that had grown irresistible under the cold weight of a decade.

"Sissy, why are you crying? Those are tears."

She wiped her eyes with her arm.

"It's the Acacia trees. It's that time of year."

He looked up at the trees, their halos of golden pollen.

"It's okay to be sad," he said. "That's what you tell me."

"I know."

"Why did the Comstock man hurt you?"

"I don't know, Joey Bear. Maybe he thought he could is all. People like that, with all the money in the world, they're used to doing whatever they want while folks look the other way. They think they own everyone, so they treat us like property. Like a toy they can break when they're angry."

"He doesn't own us," said Joe.

"He doesn't own anything, now."

They continued along the coyote trail through the tanoaks and acacias where hairy gray scat lay in the dirt and the sound of water could be heard in the southward draw. Claire steered over roots and ruts and stony washouts. Sometimes it took both of them to heave the wheelbarrow over a poor section of the trail, and the Comstock man's body would jostle side to side like a drunk in a taxicab. Soon the redwoods closed around them, and the air grew cool. They trundled along another small trail toward a sandstone outcropping that tilted out of the soil, and where it rose, it left a dark cave angling down into the earth.

"The Bunny Cave," said Joe. He'd once dropped a plush Bugs Bunny into the hole and nearly died trying to go after it. It had taken all Claire's strength and guile to pull him back from the brink. Even though it was almost ten years ago, it felt like no time had passed. "Let's say hello to Bugs. Can we say hello?"

"There's no time for that," said Claire. She maneuvered the wheelbarrow to the rim of the cave and tipped the handles so the body balled onto the edge. "We have to hurry back to Ma. And we have to clean up the yard so it stays a secret. Now, help me pull him out. Careful—don't slip."

The body lay shouldered on the lip of the wheelbarrow, one arm dangling into the blackness. Some of the blood had drained down his neck and stained the collar of his dress shirt. They stood silent for a moment, then Claire fished out his wallet and keys. She found a hundred dollars in twenties and a folded black and white photo of a naked woman posing on a couch. A girlfriend maybe, or prostitute. She returned the photo to the wallet and flung it into the hole.

Joe was watching her.

"It's for Ma's medicine," she said, slipping the cash into her bra.

"The good medicine or the pain medicine?"

"I told you, all they have for her is pain medicine. Sometimes the only thing left is to treat the pain, and the best medicine is what makes it go away the fastest. It's an act of mercy. Come on, let's get this over with."

They each took a leg and pushed the body headfirst over the rim of the cave pit. The angle lay steep and slick—gravity did most of the work for them. When the body slipped away, Joe stood with Bill's dress shoe in his hand, surprised at how eagerly the cave had taken what they'd offered. There was a brief silence, followed by a more distant thud. Claire took the shoe and tossed it into the hole, contemplating for a moment how easily lives are shunted into and out of this world.

"Say hi to Bugs," said Joe, with his hands cupped, making a small megaphone to shout through. "Tell him I'm sorry for dropping him."

***

They returned home to find Ma in anguish.

She'd kicked the covers to the floor and was hanging halfway off the bed when Claire rushed in and gently rolled her over.

"Oh Ma, what happened?"

A pair of heavy yellow eyes peered up at her. Claire noticed that Ma's gums were turning black and from her throat came ragged breaths like backwards snores. She brought down the medicine bottle from the top of the dresser and spooned the morphine gently down her throat. Ma choked it down.

"I'm going to give you extra today, okay Ma?" said Claire. She wasn't sure Ma could register what was being said. "We did some work for the Comstocks and earned enough for another bottle."

After a moment, Ma said: "Good."

Claire prepared the second spoonful and helped her take it. There wasn't much more in the bottle. Maybe another dose—or half of one. Then she filled a pot with warm water and washed Ma's face and neck. She thought of what they'd left in the Comstock's backyard—the stolen items, the broken window, *all that blood.*

Ma found Claire's hand and held it.

"You'll look after him, won't you?"

"I looked after you and Pa," said Claire. "Why wouldn't I look after Joey?"

"I know. Just want you to say it."

Ma's old eyes searched for Claire but could hardly find her.

"I will always look after him. He's all I have left."

"This world," said Ma, but she couldn't finish the thought. "Lord, this world."

"I know, Ma. I know."

She heard a voice out front—a man's voice, calling. She set down the pot and went to the window. It was Victor, the oldest Comstock brother. Not nearly as strange and sinister as his little brother, but no less arrogant. He was confronting Joe, asking him urgent questions and growing more frustrated with every word.

"Is something wrong?" said Claire, when she opened the door.

"Oh, I'd say so," said Victor. "Were you up at the house this morning?"

"No, sir. Just tending to my mother. She's very ill."

This didn't register with Victor. He held one finger aloft, pointing vaguely in the direction of the big house.

"I was supposed to meet my brother this morning," he said. "His car's here but I couldn't find him anywhere. So I go into the backyard and there's our valuable belongings laid out on the fresh-cut lawn like a goddamn garage sale."

"I wouldn't know about that," she said. "Maybe he's in the house?"

Joe stood with his big eyes tracking back and forth.

"Don't you think I looked? Thing is, after I walked out on that back lawn, I left bloody footprints on the walkway." Victor lifted his shoe to show the blood in the treads. "Do you see this? I saw the lawnmower and thought you had an accident, but here you are just fine and my brother is nowhere to be found. Now I'm wondering exactly whose blood is on my shoe. So unless you got anything to tell me, I'm calling the Sheriff to help sort it out."

Joe put his hands atop his head. "Oh, darn it all. *Darn it, darn it.*"

"What's the idiot talking about?" said Victor. He'd run out of patience—if he'd ever had any to begin with. "I demand to know what's going on."

Claire told Joe to go inside and sit with Ma, and that he could watch the new television the Comstocks had *so generously given them*. Then she turned to Victor and explained in a grave and conciliatory voice how she had just lied to him and she was about to call for an ambulance. She told him how Joe and Bill had a misunderstanding and it got physical, and Bill had fallen and hit his head on the lawn mower. She told him there was a lot of blood and it had scared her. It was the truth, mostly. And half-truths always made the best lies.

"I knew that ape had something to do with it," said Victor, stooping to look through the window of their quarters.

"He's not an ape," said Claire. "Please don't say that."

"So where is he, then? *Where the fuck is Bill?*"

She glanced over her shoulder to make sure Joe wasn't listening.

"He's still unconscious. My brother took him into the redwoods with the wheelbarrow and left him there. He was trying to hide what he'd done. I just saw for myself and ran back to call an ambulance and gather up some bandages like I said."

"Jesus Christ. You told me you didn't know what happened."

"I panicked when I saw you. I think he'll be okay—just knocked out like I said."

Victor Comstock went to the wheelbarrow and ran his finger along the rim, working the greasy blood between his thumb and forefinger. Claire imagined what he could be thinking, all the terrible things he had in store for her little family—what was left of it, anyway. Victor was just as cruel as his younger brother, but he didn't arrive at his cruelty so quickly. It built within him—a cold vindictiveness that struck at his time of choosing.

"Call the ambulance," he said, lighting a cigarette with his bloody fingers. "Then take me to him. Bring the wheelbarrow."

"Of course," she said. "I'll be right out."

***

She loaded the wheelbarrow with fresh linens and rubbing alcohol and led Victor Comstock down the coyote trail and into the dark of the redwoods. It was late morning, sunlight falling slantwise through the heavy branches. The warm, medicinal scent of redwood needles filled the air. They didn't speak a word to each other. She brought him into the small clearing beside the sandstone formation and stopped, waiting for him to speak first.

He stood blinking with his palms upturned.

"So where the hell is he?" They'd taken the trail fast, and he was nearly out of breath, sweat beading on his forehead and rolling down his jaw. "Where's my little brother?"

"We never minded living in your shadow, Victor. You should know that. We never had much at all, but we were happy growing up in the redwoods. Happy to tend the property for pennies. Long as we had each other. That's all that really mattered to me—that's all that matters today. Nothing about that has changed."

Victor took her by the shoulders and shook.

"Where the fuck is he?"

Claire pointed to the cave. "There. Joe put him in there."

"In the cave?"

"Yes. It's very deep so please watch your step."

He stepped to the rim of the cave and peered down into the blackness. A *V* of sweat bled through his dress shirt and the thin fabric clung to him like cellophane. Claire was sweating too, but for a different reason. The way he stood, quietly pondering among the great redwoods, she wondered if he could sense what was about to happen. He was about to say something when Claire slipped Pa's Smith and Wesson from her jacket pocket and fired into the back of his skull. His head pitched forward and recoiled back again and he crumpled along the very edge of the cave pit. She'd hoped he'd tumble in so it would all be over with. Instead, he lay sprawled and twitching as blood geysered from the hole in his head, darkening the redwood needles.

She took his wallet and keys and found another hundred dollars in the billfold. Then she placed the ball of her heel between Victor's shoulder blades and sent him tumbling into the hole. As she turned back to the trail, her stomach cramped, and she vomited over a bed of redwood sorrel. When she caught her breath, she wiped her face with the fresh linens and glanced at the sandstone pit and wondered just how many rich men it would take to fill it to the brim.

Hundreds, she thought.

Maybe thousands.

***

She hosed the blood from the lawnmower and scrubbed the bloody footprints from the walkway with a push broom and laundry soap. Flies were collecting in the grass where Bill Comstock had bled out and she watered that spot until the gore soaked into the dirt below. She did her best to replace the divots his boots had made as he kicked for his life. In the afternoon, she rode her bicycle two miles into town and bought another bottle of morphine solution for Ma at the pharmacy on Center Street. When she returned, she found Joe sitting with Ma, head lying on her shoulder.

"She asleep?" asked Claire.

Joe looked up at her and laid his head back down.

"Yes. She's a sleepyhead."

"I'm going to show you how to give her medicine, okay?"

"Why?"

"Because I need your help, Joey. The Comstocks asked me to sell their cars up in the city where I can get a good price. It's going to take a day to drive up and ride the bus back."

"They're not mad at me?"

"No, they're not mad at you."

"The older brother was mad."

"Not anymore. As long as I sell their cars and get a good price, they'll be happy. That's why I need your help again. When Ma starts fussing, I need you to give her a spoonful of medicine. Two at the most. I'll show you how—it's almost like feeding a baby."

Joe snorted. "I never fed a baby either."

"Well, it's good to learn. Maybe someday you'll be an *Uncle* Joey, and I'll need your help spoon-feeding my baby."

He laughed again. "You're having a baby? I didn't know."

"No, silly." She hugged him tight and kissed the top of his head. She was crying now, and she wasn't sure which of her many worries had triggered it. Maybe all of them at once. "I said someday."

***

Ma passed in her sleep two days later. Three days after that, a sheriff's deputy came knocking at their door. He was tall and serious with a trimmed blond mustache and a wide-brimmed hat that had been waterproofed so the rain beaded along the brim like tiny glass marbles. His name patch said Donnelly.

Claire invited him in, but he only stood in the doorway with his hat on.

"Wouldn't want to muddy your floor," he said. He nodded to the urn on the kitchen table, just a plain white ceramic vase with no markings or patterns. Something you might store flour in. "Sorry for your loss."

"Thank you," said Claire.

Joe wandered into the room and froze when he saw the deputy. Donnelly tipped his hat, but didn't smile.

"Wondering if you've seen any activity up at the Comstock house over the past few days?" said Donnelly. "Any cars coming and going? Anybody at all."

Claire told him she hadn't, but they'd likely been too busy worrying about their mother to notice. She said the last time she'd seen anyone was several weeks ago.

"And you, son?"

"The squirrels are soaking wet today," said Joe. Claire had instructed him to talk about squirrels if anyone asked questions about the big house. It was one of his favorite topics, and it made an easy ruse. "They've been hiding their acorns all winter so now they're big and fat. Fat for the hawks."

The deputy didn't know what to say to this.

"You all have a telephone?" he said.

"It's only good till the end of the month," said Claire. "Now that Ma's passed, we're headed back east."

"Got family out there, I take it?"

"Yes sir."

He gave a slow nod and studied the suitcases that were clammed open on the living room rug. The empty shelves, barren walls. He ran his finger down the jamb and gathered a moonlet of acacia pollen, studied it.

"Truth be told, we're looking for the Comstock brothers," he said. "William and Victor. Could be they're just living it up somewhere. I heard they like to spend time up in Reno. But if you see them around, please drop me a line. Even if you don't, I'd sure appreciate a forwarding address. Just want to make sure they're all right."

"Right as rain," said Joe, with a big grin. "Like fat squirrels."

"Yes sir," said the deputy, tipping his hat to leave. "Like fat squirrels."

***

It took nearly a week to cross the continent by bus. Claire found a nursing job in Port St. John, just a few miles from Cape Canaveral. It was enough for a tiny trailer with a propane stove and hot water, but not much more. She used the money from the Comstock's cars to buy an older model Ford, and on launch days, they would watch Delta B rockets lift over the cape atop bright, fiery clouds, and Joe would draw them in his little sketch book as they *blasted off.* On the day Kennedy was killed, Joe fell to pieces. He tore up his sketchbook and balled the colorful pages in his hands. He took it harder than when Ma and Pa passed. Harder than Bill Comstock's gruesome demise. He hit himself in the forehead with the balled-up paper and screamed *darn it, darn it, darn it,* until she was certain the neighbors could hear. It took all she had to keep him from running out the front door. But soon he came around to the possibility that maybe Kennedy wasn't really dead, that somehow he'd slipped off onto one of those big shiny rocketships and was keeping track of things from above. He was a secret astronaut, after all, and all that assassination talk was likely part of the undercover operation. Oddly enough, it wasn't the wildest theory out there. And if she ever felt guilty about shielding him from the unpredictability of death, she'd remind herself that not everything in this world has a cure, and sometimes the best medicine is whatever kills the pain.

The Breakwater Club

T he night clerk had the telephone to her ear when the man walked in, and as he neared the reception desk, she held out a finger to signal it would be a minute.

"I'm sorry, ma'am," she was saying into the receiver. She had an edge to her voice but kept the conversation professional. "I've checked twice. That's not on our list of approved emotional support animals. You might try the Beachcomber down the street."

The man set his bags on the floor and took a comb from his back pocket and ran it through his shiny black hair. His nose looked to have been broken recently and there were scaly patches on his jaw and cheeks the way heavy smokers look. He put the comb away and watched the night clerk patiently. A minute passed, and he unpocketed a silver flask from his jacket and brought it to his lips.

"I'm sorry ma'am," the night clerk continued. It sounded like she was trying to end the phone call politely. "Well, that's too bad. I'm sorry you feel that way. Right. Well, you have a lovely night." She set the phone in its cradle and stared at her desk, eyes flat and directionless. Then she glanced at the man and asked him if he had a reservation.

"No reservation," he said. "I saw the vacancy sign outside and I remembered staying here quite a few years back. Hoping to get a room with a view of the street for a couple nights."

"Shouldn't be a problem. Most want an ocean view."

"They can have it," he said, and deposited the flask into the pocket of his corduroy jacket. "After dark, it don't look like much anyhow."

"ID?"

He found his wallet and handed her a Nevada ID with the name of Emmett Krebbs, 4671 Chipwood Drive. She took it and entered the information into the computer and then she asked for all the customary details.

"Can I use a prepaid card for the hold?" he asked.

"Yes, but I have to run it first."

She ran the card and handed everything back to him, still clacking on the keyboard.

"Your eyes are crazy blue," he said. "Like a pilot light."

She paused, but didn't look up from her work. "A pilot light?"

"You know. From a wall heater, or the burner on a stove."

"First time I've heard that."

"Shit, I'm sorry. I shouldn't have said anything." He rubbed his eyes with the palms of his hands and quietly laughed to himself. His cheeks flushed. "I say the darndest things. Sometimes I surprise myself."

She gave him a keycard in a paper slip and wrote 312 over the top of it with a black sharpie pen. "Take the elevator to the third floor, then go straight down the hall," she said. "Your room is just across from the ice machine. Have a good stay, Mr. Krebbs."

"Thank you. Is the Breakwater Club open for drinks?"

"No, sorry. They'll open again at noon tomorrow."

He picked up his bags and started toward the elevator lobby, then stopped.

"One last thing," he said. "What kind of animal was that woman trying to bring in?"

Her blue eyes flashed up at him. "The lady on the phone just now?"

"Yeah, while I was waiting."

"It was some kind of weasel."

"No shit?"

"I'm not kidding," she said, trying not to smile.

"An emotional support weasel?"

"That's what she said. Said it was the reincarnation of her late husband."

He shook his head. "I've just about heard it all."

***

He unlocked the door to 312 and set his bag at the foot of the queen bed. He went to the window and looked out with his arms crossed, standing so close that his breath steamed up the glass. Headlights filtered through the late-night fog down below, winding along West Cliff Drive toward the beachside amusement park south of the hotel. If there was a moon somewhere tangled up in all that fog, he couldn't tell. He watched the parking lot below. Gauzy streetlamps. Tourist trash tumbling over the asphalt. He sat on the bed with his head in his hands for a long while and then he unzipped the duffle and placed a bottle of Jack Daniel's and a bronze-framed photograph on the writing desk. It was a holiday photo of his family in front of the Bellagio Fountains in Las Vegas. The light from the fountains backlit their profiles and made everyone look somewhat glamorous.

He found a pad of hotel stationery and an ink pen with the hotel's name on it and he took a heavy pull from the whiskey bottle and hunched crookedly over the desk and began to write.

Dear Corinne,

What they been saying about me on the news is true. Most of it, anyways. I didn't mean for it to happen. You know where my heart is. If anybody in the world knows me it's you. I shouldn't have been on the road and I know you warn me about my drinking all the time but you also know what a good driver I am. They weren't in the crosswalk like the news says. They got that part wrong. Those teenagers were goofing around in the road and throwing water balloons and the big one was pushing the little one into the street. But I know I wasn't good to drive. That's on me. I think about them like our own children and my heart breaks for their mother and father. But I just can't go away for that long. I think it might be fifteen years if I looked it up correctly. That's fifteen for each of them. I could never do that kind of time and I couldn't put you through that. I love you and the kids to the moon and back and I am very sorry.

Love, Emmett.

He read the letter twice through, and when he was satisfied, he removed a silver folding knife from his duffle and unfolded the blade and locked it open. He pinned the note to the wall with the knifetip and stepped back to read it a third time.

"Goddamn," he whispered. "Feels like a dream."

He brought the bottle into the bathroom and shut the door gently behind him. He flicked on the fan and spun the shower knob and popped the diverter from the tub spout so the water hissed and sputtered through the shower head. He undressed and left his clothes in a pile. From the pocket of his sweatshirt, he removed a pack of Camel Lights and lit one with a gas station lighter. He stood there naked and smoking while the shower steamed and the water gurgled into the drain. He sensed his own reflection in the mirror, but he didn't turn to look at himself. Eventually he climbed into the shower with the stream wetting his back and he stood smoking and drinking until he was very drunk. The mirror had fogged over by then and when he finally stepped out of the tub, he could only make out a phantom outline of himself in the glass. He watched his blurred form, tilting left and right. Taking sloppy pulls from the bottle. With his finger he drew devil horns on his foggy reflection and stepped back to fit himself into the outline. He stared at his devil-self in the mirror until his eyes and the world uncoupled and he could no longer keep himself standing.

***

He woke the next morning atop the bedspread with a bath towel wrapped around his waist and the pillows on the floor. He'd nearly drained the whiskey and was out of cigarettes. He looked at the digital clock on the bedside table. Just past ten o'clock. He got dressed, combed his hair, and went to the window. The fog hadn't cleared, and it didn't look like it was going to. In the distance he could just make out the Santa Cruz Mountains. Redwoods cascading down the San Lorenzo Valley, slipping into gossamer. A trolley bus materialized from the fog and deposited a dozen tourists onto the street corner, and he watched them shuffle off in all directions—some down Beach Street and others toward the Municipal Wharf.

He looked at the note he'd tacked to the wall, but it hurt his eyes to read it. Last night's booze riled the optic nerves. Instead, he pocketed the knife and folded the note into his breast pocket. He drank the rest of the whiskey in three noisy breaths. Before he left the room he brought out a charcoal-colored 9mm pistol from his duffle and laid it on the bed. He considered it a long while. He went back and forth to the window, alternately gazing at the fogged-out world and the pistol. Finally, he stuffed the gun into the front pocket of his sweatshirt and left the room.

***

He crossed the lobby and went through the double doors and out to the street. The air was cold and smelled like tide pools and car exhaust. He could hear a foghorn droning somewhere across the bay. There were women passing on the sidewalk wearing bikinis and laughing to each other as if they were in some kind of tropical parallel universe where the sun was shining. At the corner of Beach and Front Street sat a liquor store with neon beer signs in the windows and he walked that way across the roundabout and went inside. He went past aisles filled with snacks and warm cases of beer to the counter in back where an old man sat on a stool, staring at a small TV. On the screen, a weatherman waved his arms at a map of the west coast and revealed his prediction for tomorrow's temperatures throughout the region.

Emmett stood watching the old man expectantly until he rose from his stool and shuffled to the counter.

"Camel Lights."

The man nodded and reached above his head where an assortment of cigarette packs had been divided into a display rack. He wriggled one out from the rack and set it on the counter.

"Nine dollars and sixty cents," he said.

Emmett stood with a surprised look. "Nine dollars?"

"Yessir," said the old man. "And sixty cents."

"Is this a California thing?"

"Last I checked."

Emmett gave a long whistle. He sorted through his wallet and found a ten-dollar bill and laid it on the plexiglass counter.

"These must be those new cigarettes that make your wife fall in love with you again and your lost dog come running back," he said.

The man shook his head. "They're just regular cigarettes. But they're taxed straight up your colon. You from out of state, friend?"

"Nevada."

"That right? Whereabouts in Nevada? We've got a little place in Tahoe just across the state line."

Emmett looked up at the television. His face briefly appeared over a chyron that read: ON THE RUN. He was surprised that he'd made national news. He was about to tell the old man where he was from when another man stormed in and went straight for the beer coolers. He was muttering to himself. Late forties, blond hair pasted to his forehead in a greasy fan. A beard like a civil war general. His eyes looked hard and distant as if he were sleepwalking. He swung open the cooler doors and wrestled two forty-ounce bottles of Olde English from the cooler racks and then he fled out the front doors without making eye contact.

"Goddamn you! I told you not to come back," shouted the shopkeeper, but he made no effort to chase him. He counted the change for the cigarettes and scooted it across the plexiglass with a contemptuous look.

"That happen a lot?" said Emmett.

"It happens. One of these days I'll shoot the motherfucker."

"You'd shoot him for that?"

"Why the hell not? I got the right, don't I?"

"I don't think that's true. Just looked like a regular ol' bum to me. There's bums everywhere."

"Exactly. Nobody would miss him."

"See, you don't know that," Emmett bristled. "He had to come from somewhere. Somebody named him. Maybe that somebody thinks about him from time to time. Or maybe he was raised rough, and it broke something down deep that he could never fix."

The old man gave a disappointed look and shook his head.

"Maybe you should run for city council. You'd fit right in with all the damn bleeding hearts."

Emmett spun the pull-tab on the cigarette pack and left the plastic film recoiling on the countertop. He tapped out a smoke and raised it to his lips.

"Just saying it ain't worth a man's life."

"A man?"

"Yes sir. You saying he ain't one?"

"Maybe he used to be."

"Buddy, you better listen up. Your humanity don't end when the luck runs out."

The old man had enough.

"Just get the fuck out. You can't smoke in here anyhow."

***

He leaned on the wharf railings, smoking and watching the beach fill with tourists. The tide was in, four-foot shore breaks. Sea spray blew in with the fog and it looked like a giant cloud had settled on the beach. Optimists opened umbrellas and pitched camping tents as if charming the sunshine. He stood there a long while until his wristwatch read noon and then he wandered back to the hotel and through the doors of The Breakwater Club.

He found a seat at the corner of the rectangular bar and sat so he could watch the waves. He was the first customer of the day. The bartender came in from the kitchen and gave a friendly nod. A good-looking college kid with light stubble and silver earrings. He placed a square napkin on the bar and asked what he'd be having.

"I spent my honeymoon here," said Emmett. "Twenty years ago in July."

The kid didn't know why he was telling him this, but it didn't faze him.

"We've had a few remodels since then, I bet."

"It don't look much different. Same amount of fog in the windows, I guess that don't change."

"People think California is sunny in the summertime. They don't expect the June gloom." The kid caught himself. "No offense to you, sir. It's an honest mistake."

"You got to do worse to offend me, son."

"So, what can I get you?"

"Twenty years ago this place carried a bottle of Pappy Van Winkle, and it was selling for thirty dollars a glass. The bartender was bragging about it so I ordered one. Been thinking about it ever since."

The kid gave a little smile as if he were about to tell a secret.

"Well, you are in luck, my friend. We still carry it. The rich techies from San Jose order a glass from time to time. It costs a little more now, of course."

"I can taste it already."

"So, you'll have a glass?"

"Just bring the whole bottle down."

The kid played it cool. "I can arrange that." He climbed to the top step of a three-step ladder and edged the bottle carefully from the shelf. He brought it down and admired the label, blew off a thin layer of dust. "You take it neat?"

"Do you have those big round ice cubes?"

"I'm afraid not." He plucked an ice cube from a basin and held it up with a pair of tongs. "Just these little half-moon-shaped ones."

"One of those will do."

The kid plunked the ice cube into an old-fashioned glass and poured two fingers of whiskey. The ice crackled. "Do you want to start a tab?"

Emmett took a slow sip and swallowed. His eyes fluttered.

"Goddamn that's good."

"It better be at that price, am I right?" He was standing close by as if waiting for a credit card.

"I hate to do this to you, kid."

The kid's smile faded. "Hate to do what?"

Emmett laid the 9mm on the bar and gave an apologetic look.

"First of all, I'm not going to hurt you. Do you understand?"

The kid nodded. He looked like he was holding his breath.

"Tell me you understand."

"I understand."

"Good. Now I want you to call the front desk and tell them I have a gun and I'm demanding that someone close the doors to the bar so it's just you and me alone in here. Can you do that for me?"

Another nod. "You want me to do it now?"

"Yes."

Emmett drank and stared out the murky window. The kid went to a phone by the register and told the front desk what was happening and what must be done. His voice held steady—the voice of someone good in a crisis. The bar was quiet for a moment, and you could hear the waves and the shorebirds down on the beach. A motorcycle throttling down the road.

The double doors closed suddenly from the outside. Emmett didn't want to see the person's face doing the closing, so he didn't look.

"Can you turn on the TV, please?"

The kid did what he was asked. The news was on, and Emmett's face took up a third of the frame. It was an old profile picture from a social media account he never used. Beneath the photo were the words HIT AND RUN DRIVER'S TRUCK FOUND IN SANTA CRUZ, CA.

"That's you, isn't it?" said the kid, almost whispering.

"You don't have to whisper."

"I'm sorry."

"Yeah, it's me. I made a really bad mistake, and I hurt people I didn't mean to hurt. Can you pour me another round?"

The kid poured.

Emmett lit a cigarette. "Is that really how you spell your name?" he asked. He was pointing to the name tag on the kid's vest that read *J-a-c-c-o-b-b*.

"This? No. They spelled it wrong when they gave it to me. I spell it with one *c* and one *b*."

"So why do you wear it?"

"I guess I thought it was funny. Nobody really notices."

"I noticed. Names are sacred, Jacob. Sometimes it's all you have left."

"Do you want me to take it off?"

"No. I just want you to understand the power of names." He ashed his cigarette onto the paper napkin. "There's almost a magical quality to them. Does that sound crazy?"

"No, sir."

"You don't have to agree with me because you're afraid."

"Well, it sounds a little crazy I guess."

Emmett laughed, took a big sip. "I like you, Jacob. See, the thing about names is they attract dirt. You really have to work to keep them clean. And the dirtier they get, the more dirt they attract, and things really start to get bad for you. Your name can take on a permanent stain. Then you start to feel hopeless. At least that's how it is in this country. We like to talk about second chances and turn-around stories, but that's all fake. In this country you're lucky to get a chance at all, let alone a second one. What they don't tell you is that people actually want you to fail. They like to see a name get dirty. Do you want to know why?"

Jacob shrugged. "Why?"

"Because they like to know they're not among the dirty. They see someone fail and it gives them something to measure against. A reference point. My father was a sonofabitch, but he told me something that stuck. He told me never to tell anyone about your problems. Do you want to guess why?"

"Because nobody cares?"

"That's partially right. He said half don't care. The remaining half actually enjoy that you're having problems. Like I said, it makes them feel better to see someone worse off. Now I'm not saying you can't have someone special to talk to, and that's okay. Someone you trust. Maybe you talk to a shrink now and then. I've done it. But keep in mind the world is mostly cruel and hostile and wants you to fail. If you're not careful, it'll get what it wants." Emmett finished the glass and rattled the ice. "Do you have a girlfriend?"

Jacob scooped a new ice cube and gave him a hefty pour.

"A boyfriend."

"What's his name?"

He hesitated. "Do I have to tell you?"

"No, you don't."

"Then I'm not going to if it's all the same."

"That's smart. You're a smart kid. Do people tell you that?"

"Yes, sometimes."

"Well, go ahead and text him if you want. Tell him everything will be okay."

While Jacob was texting, the bar phone rang. He stopped texting and answered it. After a few words were exchanged, he pressed the phone to his vest.

"It's the police. They want to talk to you."

Emmett was drinking faster now. He was already halfway done with the latest pour.

"Tell them I won't come out no matter what."

Jacob told them. "They want to know about letting me go."

"Tell them when the bottle's through, I'll let you go."

He went to the window with the old-fashioned glass in one hand and the pistol in the other. Down on the beach, two police officers were going from group to group and waving their hands, pointing to the hotel. Everyone was leaving the beach in a hurry. Parents sheltered their children with their arms wrapped tightly around them as they ran. He returned to the bar and sat down, the television droning his name again and again.

"Mute the TV," he said. His words came out sloppy. "I don't want to hear my name anymore. I already know how this ends."

Jacob waved the remote and the TV went silent.

"How does it end?"

"With me in the ground. I've known it all along."

"They said you can surrender and see your wife and kids again."

"My wife and kids don't want to see me. They're ashamed of me."

"At least you'll live."

"Not with a name this dirty. It's no way to live, believe me."

***

Emmett was on his final glass when the phone rang again. Jacob answered and set the phone down on the bar.

"They want to know if I can go now," he said.

Emmett raised the glass and nodded to the door. He was very drunk now.

"Be gone, my friend. I bid you adieu." He set the glass down and some of the whiskey spilled over his hand. He pulled out his wallet and fumbled with the billfold. "Hold up, now. I have a tip for you. Only fifty bucks but that's all I got left in the world."

Jacob waved him off.

"You can keep it." Then, into the phone, "I'm going to come out now. It's just me, okay?" He went to the double doors and opened one of them slowly. Just a crack at first. He poked his head out and announced he was coming out again and then he left and closed the door behind him.

The phone rang immediately. Emmett didn't answer. It rang and rang and then it stopped. The fog was burning off and he could see patches of blue sky marbled in the gray. He wanted to go to the window and watch the sun come out, but he was too drunk to stand. The phone rang again. He couldn't have answered it if he wanted to. On the television, a woman appeared with dark curly hair, and he thought maybe it was Corinne. The way she stood, the way she held herself loosely when she was anxious as if the tension made her cold—he thought it must be her. His eyes watered and the world blurred. He wanted to know if she had a message for him, if she'd worked everything out with the police and wanted him to come home. He wanted nothing more than to be with her again. She'd been here in this bar with him, standing at the window with a cocktail in her hand, watching the tide come in. It didn't feel like twenty years ago. He slid off the stool to find the remote so he could hear her voice but lost his balance and fell onto his ass with the last of the whiskey spilling down his chest. He sat and wept.

A minute later, the door burst open and white smoke filled the room, voices shouting on top of each other like barking seals. Emmett raised the empty glass and the pistol to welcome the newcomers amid the clatter of rifle fire.

***

It was September the following year when Corinne Kessler approached the reception desk with large black sunglasses and an overnight bag slung over her shoulder.

"Just the one night?" asked the clerk.

"Yes, just the one night." She set down a credit card and ID and then she unfolded another piece of paper from the Social Security Office. "I know the names don't match. I started using my maiden name again. See, here?"

The clerk set everything on her desk and clacked on her keyboard and handed everything back. She wrote on the back of a key card with a black sharpie.

"You're on the top floor, Ms. Kessler. Room 418."

"Is the Breakwater Club open?" she asked.

The clerk looked that way. "Yes, but we changed the name to the *Mariner Lounge* after the remodel. They're usually open till around midnight. The jazz band is pretty good if you're into that kind of thing."

Corinne thanked her and gathered her things. She went straight to the bar without going to her room first. It was busy inside, maybe two-dozen people. Mostly couples with a few loners sitting around the bar. A jazz trio played some 1950s standard from the corner of the room. She went to the bar and asked for a glass of Pappy Van Winkle. She ordered it neat. The bartender was a middle-aged woman named Donna who wore her hair long and straight with a streak of blue.

"Do you want to start a tab?" Donna asked.

"Yes," said Corinne, and handed her a credit card.

When the drink came, she thanked the bartender and found an empty bistro table by the window. The night was clear with just a tinge of sea spray making fuzzy halos around the wharf lights. A big bright moon cast over the shore break and the seafoam looked stark in all that moonlight. She took a sip from her drink. It burned her throat a little and she let out a small cough. She drank again and unfolded the note she had kept in her purse since last summer, and when she read it, her eyes welled. She drank heavily and read it again. This time she began crying so loudly that others turned to look at her. She cried as if it were for the very first time.

"Dammit, Emmett," she was saying. "You crazy sonofabitch. You goddamn fool."

She cried until the band stopped playing. Whispers simmered all around her. The bartender came around the bar and gently put a hand on her shoulder.

"It's okay," said the bartender, as the band counted in the next song. "Everything's going to be okay."

"No, it won't," she sobbed. "Not for a lot of people. Not for me."

"Someday, then. Maybe someday it will be."

All Her Diamond Rings

Markeem was replacing the master cylinder on an early model Chevy Camaro when he sensed someone watching him. He'd always thought of the feeling like a sixth sense—a sudden coldness on the back of the neck, a faint ringing in the ears. When he was a child, his mother would say someone had *walked over his grave*. The saying never made much sense to him until she explained while he didn't have a grave, an anonymous patch of dirt existed somewhere in the world, waiting to receive him.

He set his ratchet on the tool tray and glanced around the shop. It was just past noon, and the other mechanics were out at their typical lunch spots. Bruno's BBQ, Wendy's, the noodle joint around the corner. He turned to the front of the shop and spotted a middle-aged woman standing at the open bay door. Salon hairstyle, designer purse clutched tight. The sun was at her back and he couldn't make out the face.

"Markeem Kennon?" she asked.

He went to her with a shop rag in his hand, casually scrubbing the grime from the webs of his fingers. He pointed to the cursive letters embroidered into his navy-blue shop jacket as if he'd just learned of his own identity.

"I guess that's me," he said.

"You don't remember me, do you?" she said.

The cold sensation grew as she bore her pale blue eyes upon him.

Then he knew. All at once, he knew.

"You're Jenna's mother."

She gave a small grin—just enough to let him know he'd gotten it right.

"Have you taken lunch yet?" she asked, glancing at the burger joint at the other end of the lot. "I'll buy."

"I usually eat leftovers." He stood uncomfortably, looking over her shoulder to see if she was alone. The thought occurred to him that maybe she had a gun in her purse, even though she didn't seem overtly hostile. Sad and desperate, maybe—but not hostile. "What's this about? I don't think I've seen you in fifteen—"

"It's not about Jenna. I know that's what you're thinking. Can't we just talk for a bit?"

"Your name is Valerie—or Veronica? I can't remember."

"Valerie," she said. "Robertson. It's okay that you don't remember."

He took out his phone and noted the time.

"You know what they say about free lunches," he said.

"All you have to do is listen."

***

Markeem settled into the booth with a double cheeseburger and waited for her to talk. He took a bite and chewed without taking his eyes off her. He'd seen her only once since Jenna's death, about a year afterward. Just a random encounter at a hardware store, and it wasn't a friendly exchange. She'd cornered him in the plumbing aisle and blamed him for everything: Jenna's dope habit, her homelessness, the crime sprees—her fatal overdose in the woods behind her parents' house. He'd taken her outburst with great restraint. He hadn't been entirely blameless, after all.

But neither was she.

"You taught her how to steal cars," said Valerie. All she'd ordered for herself was a small bag of fries and a soda, and she sat sipping from the straw and letting the fries get cold. "You still do any of that?"

"No, I just fix them now," he said. "Doesn't pay as well, but the cops are much friendlier. My landlady, on the other hand, she doesn't like me as much."

She made a look like she was mildly surprised.

"I see. You're on the straight and narrow."

"I try."

"Have you ever worked on a 1970 'Cuda convertible?"

"Maybe. I don't really keep a log."

"There weren't many made. The ones with the dual-quad Hemi V8 sell for over a million dollars at auction."

Markeem stopped chewing and held a wad of cheeseburger in his cheek.

"You don't strike me as a gearhead."

"No? Why not?"

"You'd ruin those beautiful diamonds, for one."

She glanced at her rings as if she'd forgotten she was wearing them.

"Well, you don't strike me as a choir boy. The world is full of surprises."

"I'm starting to feel profiled."

"Just recalling your history. *By their fruit you shall know them.*" She'd started out polite and deferential, but her tone had deteriorated quickly. "You were a thief and a druggie, and you led my daughter to an early grave."

"Having a straitjacket childhood had nothing to do with it? I hear kids love when you make them play the cello till their fingers bleed." Markeem wiped his mouth with a paper napkin, wadded it into a ball, and tossed it onto the tray. "Always a pleasure," he said, and rose.

"Wait—don't go. I deserved that. I told you I wouldn't dredge up the past—and just look at me, like I can't even help it. And it's true I don't really know a thing about cars." The sadness he'd sensed in her now felt more like loneliness, like this was the first real conversation she'd had in months and had forgotten how to do it. "The reason I asked about the car is because my husband has one and it's all he talks about. It's black and chrome—really beautiful when it's all polished up. And so rare, apparently. He brags about it to all his country club friends."

"And you're telling me why?"

"Because I want you to steal it and keep the money for yourself."

He looked around to see who might be listening.

"I told you I don't do that anymore."

"I know what you said. Did I mention it's a million-dollar car?"

***

He told her no.

He told her not to contact him again.

But he found himself lingering in the parking lot, sucking the hamburger gristle from his teeth, waiting for Valerie to come wandering out with all those diamond rings glinting in the high-noon sun. He had a cousin in Reno who could handle a classic car like that, who could arrange a private sale without drawing much attention. It wouldn't be an auction price, and it would take a few months to trickle all that money into the system. But even with a *hot car penalty*—

"Change your mind?" she said. She stood with her purse unclasped, and again he wondered about a gun, even though they were in a busy parking lot in the middle of a lunch rush. Instead, she handed him a prepaid phone still in the package. "I'll call you Friday after dinner. Make sure you charge it and keep the ringer on."

"I know how phones work," he said. "I'm more curious about the woman on the other end and what she's going to say when I ask what's in it for her?"

"I'm certain the woman will say something about her husband's public philandering and relentless verbal abuse, and how she would love nothing more than to see him humiliated and bereft of his prized possession. But you'll need to wait and ask her yourself."

***

He sat in the dark of his trailer with a can of Tecate, scrolling through television shows that felt like they were made for everyone but him. He thought of Jenna and how they'd met at that crowded downtown party all those years ago, how those first few months together were like driving the fastest car ever built—only the car had no brakes or headlights, and the only way out was through the windshield. On nights like these, he'd bring the banker's box down from the closet—the one full of artifacts he knew he shouldn't keep—and he'd stand in the kitchenette and flip the old wool ski mask inside out and search for little blond hairs under the bright stove light. Then he'd twist them between his fingers and marvel how those hairs were the last parts of her to exist in the living world, and how strange it was to weep over something so slight and ordinary.

***

She called around midnight.

He'd fallen asleep watching some old detective movie and it took until the fifth ring to answer. He still had Jenna's ski mask balled in his hand.

"You're drunk," he said—he could tell right away. "You at a bar?"

"Yes to both," she said. "A little dive on Cedar Street. First time I've been alone at a dive bar in decades. It's depressing to tell the truth. Everyone is glued to their phones, and they don't let you smoke cigarettes anymore. I guess phones are the new smoking?"

"You said you'd call after dinner."

"Couldn't get free. The old man and I really got into it this time."

"Don't make him think you hate him," said Markeem. "He'll get suspicious."

"Oh darling, he'll never put it together. I'm a hundred percent sure."

"Only fools are a hundred percent sure."

"Then I'm a hundred and ten percent sure."

He laughed. "Go on, then."

She danced around the topic, commenting on various dramas unfolding inside the bar. A spilled drink. A low-cut dress. It took Markeem a minute to steer her back to business. But after hearing the first few details of the plan, he cut her off and flatly announced he wasn't interested. He wasn't even polite about it.

"You're describing a carjacking," he said, pulling the tab on his last can of beer. "It's a violent felony—and probably the worst goddamn way to steal a car. It's the way tweakers do it."

"Wait, wait, wait, don't hang up," she said. "There's two parts of this you gotta know. One, I absolutely have to see the precious look on his face when you march him out of the car at gunpoint. I want to see him completely powerless for a change. That part's a deal-breaker. But I thought you'd feel strongly about it—and obviously I was right—so the second part is a bit of a pot sweetener."

"It's hard to imagine a pot sweet enough, to be honest."

"We'll be attending Burt Schlosinger's gala at the country club that night. I don't expect you to know who that is, but he's turning ninety and he wants to go out with a bang. So lucky for you, that means I'll be wearing all my diamonds. You commented on them the other day. But there will also be a necklace, earrings, and a bracelet. If my diamond brooch works with my dress, I'll wear that too. I'll be practically begging for it."

"Give me a figure. I'm not a pawn shop."

"They're insured for half a million if that helps. I'm sure he'll wear his Rolex, too. Exactly how sweet do you want the pot to be?"

"And he'll have the top down on the convertible?"

"I'll insist on it. I have a riding scarf and everything. So?"

A long pause, then: "Maybe."

"Maybe? The Gala's next Saturday night. You won't have long to think about it."

"It's risky—and I don't trust you."

"Believe me. The only risk will be whether my husband shits himself in the driver seat and lowers the value of the car." He could hear her ordering another drink from the bartender.

Sounded like a gin and tonic with lime. When she came back on, her voice chirped with a sudden hiccup. "As for trust, I don't know what to tell you. I don't have time to go up the trust curve with you."

"You have a reason to set me up. To send me away."

"Yes, that's true. But lately I've been wondering about Jenna's time with you, those last couple years. I think about it more and more. My husband and I kept her caged and she ran straight for you the second she broke free—but at least she was free. That's how I've been thinking about it, lately. Maybe I wouldn't say this if I wasn't already four cocktails deep, but she wasn't safe in the cage, either."

"Safe from whom? Your husband?"

Markeem couldn't tell if the sounds coming through the phone were hiccups or covert sobs. Jenna hated her mother and never said a kind word about her, but she never mentioned her father. Markeem had asked once if he was even alive and she'd replied: *God I wish he wasn't.*

"Still there?" said Markeem. He took a long sip of beer and waited.

"I just want to see that stupid face of his when you point the gun at him," said Valerie, and he was sure she was crying now. "That's what this is all about. I want to see him at your mercy. Weak. Powerless. Afraid. And I really do hope he makes a mess of that stupid car."

***

The next day, Markeem tailed her.

He'd spotted her silver Mercedes wheeling down the country road just a mile from her six-bedroom trophy house in the Santa Cruz Mountains and slipped in behind her. He followed her into town, all the way to the harbor where she stopped at an up-scale nail salon called Sea Wind Boutique. It was warm, maybe eighty-five degrees, and she wore a silk dress with a woven sun hat and dark glasses. He wanted to get a better sense of her, to see if he could gather enough red flags to blow her off for good. He wouldn't need much—he almost had enough reasons as it was—but he'd never heard of a pot so big for so little work and he was struggling to keep the fantasy in check.

After the nail salon, she bought a liter of booze from an east side liquor store and drove to Oak Wood Cemetery where she poured half the bottle into a canteen and wandered down a stone-lined path to a shady wrought-iron bench. Markeem knew Jenna was buried here, although he'd never visited. He found the notion of standing six feet above an audience of well-dressed corpses too macabre to have any therapeutic value. Besides, Jenna wouldn't have wanted to be trapped in a dark box for all eternity. It was the reason she'd run to him, after all.

It was the reason she'd kept running.

He sat watching Valerie for an hour or so, until she passed out with her head tilted and lips parted, shoulders rising and falling peacefully. He stepped out of the car and slipped on his sunglasses. The cemetery felt abandoned. There was a pair of ravens dipping their heads atop the older stones on the far side of the property, clacking and calling. He went slowly along the path and sat beside Valerie. She didn't wake. He could hear her breath rattling softly in her throat. Her purse sat beside her, and he set it on his lap and looked inside. A snakeskin wallet. A bottle of pepper spray. Makeup. Towelettes. He found four prescription bottles for Xanax, Klonopin, Vicodin, and Ativan—all nearly empty.

"What else you got in here?" he whispered, amused.

Inside a zippered pocket sat a little gray Ruger with a ten-round magazine.

He peeked at the chambered round and returned the gun to the purse.

It felt good to be right.

He slipped the cell phone from her slack fingers and held it to her face and unlocked it. He read her texts, her emails. He spent ten minutes thumbing through the photos in her photo library and then he clicked the phone to black and rested it on the bench and left.

***

She called two nights later—this time at one in the morning.

He was up watching television, waiting for the call.

"I wondered if you'd even pick up," she said. "So, what's the verdict?"

She sounded drunker than last time.

"I'll do it," said Markeem. "But I'm the only one with a gun, understand? If that little Ruger of yours comes out to play, you'll be sorry."

"I'll be sorry? Don't speak to me like a child. I don't even own a gun."

"Deny it again and I'll hang up. I followed you a couple days ago and looked through your purse while you were on the nod. I looked through your phone, too. It was enlightening."

"I wondered where all my pills went. What else did you find?"

"I found inspirational screengrabs about loneliness. Solo dinners at the golf course. Birthdays and anniversaries that passed without celebration. I found a pill-popping alcoholic. A woman with a cruel and egotistical husband who ignores her texts for days on end only to give a one word reply or a middle-finger emoji when he does respond. I found *you*, Valerie."

A long pause.

Ice chiming in the glass.

She exhaled, then: "Is that all?"

"No," he said. "I also found a woman whose story checks out."

***

Markeem parked the tractor trailer on a fire road about a quarter mile from the Robertson's property. He wore a yellow hardhat with sunglasses and a black dust mask. Long sleeves and nylon gloves to cover his tattoos. It was another hot day, and by the time he reached the long dirt driveway, he could feel sweat gathering at his temples and running down the back of his neck. He set out an orange cone at the egress of the driveway and waited. Only two trucks passed on the country road, and when they did, he'd turn and kick at a plastic drainage pipe at the bottom of the driveway and study it as if it somehow needed studying.

Soon, he heard the telltale rumble of a V8 Hemi, some Kenny Rogers song playing loud on the stereo. When the car neared, Markeem stepped out with one hand in the air and the other flat on his front pocket, concealing the grip of his 9mm pistol. The 'Cuda's top was down as Valerie promised it would be, and she sat in the passenger seat, her hair up in a riding scarf. Black gown, diamonds from head to toe. Her husband wore a tuxedo with French cuffs. Markeem could see the Rolex on his wrist as he prepared to turn onto the country road.

Instead, the car slowed, and the V8 sat idling like a motorboat.

Black and chrome and sleek and beautiful.

"We don't have time for this shit," said the husband. He waved his hand at the orange cone and pushed a phony berm of hair up his scalp. "What are you idiots even working on down here?"

Markeem raised the gun.

"Out of the car. Both of you. Keep the engine running."

"Are you fucking kidding me?" said the husband. He huffed and gave a look like *you can't do this to me*. But fear quickly took over. He held his hands up and looked at Valerie, who was already opening the car door and stepping onto the driveway.

"Leave the jewelry," said Markeem. "The watch, too. Hurry."

The main road was clear, but he kept checking anyway.

Valerie stripped her jewelry and tossed it on the passenger seat. Her husband worked the Rolex over his manicured hand. He was watching Markeem with a sort of dumb paralysis, working his jaw like he wanted to say something but could not. Maybe this was the look she wanted to see.

Markeem thumbed the handle and pulled open the car door. Then he re-trained the Glock on the man's forehead to ratchet the fear a notch or two.

"Out. *Now!*"

Valerie came creeping around the back of the car. He knew she wanted to see her husband's face better, but he couldn't have her flanking him like that. She wasn't even pretending to be scared—eyes hard and hungry.

He thought he saw the edges of a smile.

"Stay where you are," he warned her.

But now she had that little gray pistol in her hand, pointed at her husband.

"You're a monster, Ted," she told him. "Hell isn't hot enough for what you did to Jenna and me."

"Valerie, what are you—"

She fired twice.

Her husband clapped a hand over his throat as the shots spread over the desolate countryside. The pristine collar of his tuxedo shirt reddened. His mouth made an oval and his eyes bared their wormy pink veins. His other hand raised up and pinched at the air as if trying to give some kind of signal, almost like wanting a check at a restaurant, then blood fountained from his lips and he fell through the open door choking and sputtering on the driveway.

Valerie tossed the gun into the backseat along with her silk gloves and raised her hands in surrender. In her eyes was a malevolent look of satisfaction.

"You set me up," said Markeem, inching away from the dying man to avoid the blood spatter. He had the Glock trained on her, working the angles in his mind.

Shooting her wasn't at the bottom of his list of options.

"I used you," she said. "But I didn't set you up."

"They'll know your Ruger is missing. They'll check your firearm records."

"It was in my purse. You took it with you. That's all they need to know."

He stepped forward, both hands on the gun.

Bearing down on her.

"And what did I look like?"

"A skinny red-haired man with meth scabs." She glanced at the little stream of blood snaking through the grooves of the paving stones and motioned to the car as if inviting him to take a ride. "I told you, it's not a set-up. You helped me get what I want and now here is your payment—and my alibi."

Markeem studied her, and what he'd thought was satisfaction now looked something like relief. She looked like a woman who had just found a lost child in a crowded store or received good news about an illness.

"Give me five goddamn minutes before calling it in," he said. "I need all the headstart I can get."

She took out her phone and launched the timer app and showed him.

"Drive fast," she said. "Time's a-wastin'"

He stepped over the dying man and into the driver seat of the 'Cuda. He threw the transmission into gear and swerved around the traffic cone and roared onto the country road with the tires skirling and dust kicking up around him. He didn't look back. The sweat had soaked through his clothes, and the wind felt cool as he wheeled around the curves. He found the tractor trailer on the fire road where he'd left it with the ramp lowered, and he carefully trundled up into the back of it. A marred spot on the dashboard caught his eye, and he unfolded the buck knife from his belt and dug into the spot until a dark spall of lead fell out onto the passenger floorboard.

He recovered it and held it pinched between his gloved fingers.

The engine was loud inside the trailer.

Glug glug glug glug glu—

He killed the ignition and studied the bullet, wondering what manner of cruelty a family would have to endure to cause a daughter to flee into the arms of a criminal and a wife to murder her husband with such unrepentant glee.

***

By February, Markeem's cousin had sold the car and most of the jewelry. What his cousin couldn't get into the banks, Markeem kept in a duffle in a hidden compartment beneath his trailer where it awaited his next act—as owner of a small dive bar on the Oregon coast, soon to be reimagined as a mechanic-themed watering hole called THE TIRE IRON. It would be the kind of place with hubcaps and license plates on the walls and a jukebox that never played anything past the mid-nineties—a place for him to grow old while surrounded by sea fog and a few hundred gallons of cold beer.

He was packing what little he owned into cardboard boxes when he felt that old icy feeling on the back of his neck, the faint ringing sound like mosquito wings. He looked up and found her standing in the doorway. He didn't recognize her right away—she'd lost weight, and her department store clothes looked worn and discolored. The salon hairstyle had gone flat and an inch of silver grew along her hairline.

"You shouldn't be here," said Markeem.

The air was frigid, and her breath steamed as she stood watching him with a strange, withered smile. She shuffled to the couch and sat. The slow, fluid movement of her eyes screamed full-blown junkie.

"Nobody's following me if that's what you're worried about," she said.

He rose and pointed to the door with the box cutters in his hand.

"Look at you," he said. "Genghis Khan could have followed you on a unicycle and you wouldn't have noticed. Leave, Valerie. I don't want to ask again."

She opened her purse. Markeem was prepared to take cover behind the kitchen counter, but she only removed a near-empty soft pack of Camel 100s and placed the wrong end of a long white cigarette between her teeth before languidly turning it around. She flicked a lighter and chased it with the tip of the smoke.

"You thought I was going to shoot, huh?" she said, amused.

"I've seen you do it before."

"We're long past that, don't you think? That reminds me—they picked someone up for our little crime. Thought you'd want to know."

"I didn't hear about an arrest."

"You will. Maybe tomorrow. Somebody robbed the 7-Eleven on Laurel Street and had the right color hair and meth scars. I guess they cornered him in some downtown alleyway—at least that's what Chief Mills tells me. Sounds like the cops like him for it. I know the DA wants to put this whole thing to bed in a hurry."

"Is that why you're here?"

"Not really."

"Tell me what you want and leave."

She twisted the cap off a bottle of pills and palmed them into her mouth. A pint of cheap vodka teetered up and down like a louver. She made a sound like it hurt to swallow, but it also sounded like a welcome pain.

"I started chasing airplanes," she said. She'd left her purse on the couch and wandered toward the open door as if she might see a plane. "After the thrill of killing Ted wore off, I got bored. It wore off faster than I thought it would. I started watching those commercial jet planes flying low in the sky and wondering where they were headed. I'm terrified of flying, and I'm jealous of people who aren't. I started following them in my car as far as I could, just to see how far I could get. A little farther each time. I wouldn't have cared if I ended up plunging into the Pacific Ocean." She paused to look at her ringless fingers, as if she'd forgotten where they'd gone. "Then I caught one. It must have been flying slower than the rest. It was Christmas morning, and the roads were empty. I drove fast—dangerously fast. I thought I was going to die, but I didn't care."

Markeem stood with his arms folded.

A part of him was starting to feel sorry for her.

"Where was it going?" he asked.

"Nowhere. It landed here at the airport. It turned out none of the planes I was chasing were going anywhere interesting at all. They were all coming back home. Can you imagine that? Just a sad old lady chasing planes going nowhere at all."

"I don't understand why you're telling me any of this."

"She's alive, Markeem."

They locked eyes.

She had the same look of relief as the day she killed her husband.

"Who's alive?"

"Who do you think? The love of our lives. She wanted to get clean so she got Ted to pay for some platinum-tier rehab overseas. Then she made him buy her a grave plot with a tombstone and a death date. We even put out an obituary in the paper. She wanted a clean break from all her junkie friends. Including you."

"You're lying."

"We didn't have a choice. She threatened to tell the police everything he'd done to her all those years. She had proof. Enough to make the whole thing work, to force her father to go along." She sent her cigarette pinwheeling onto the driveway and lit another. "I found her online a few weeks ago. She looks healthy. Married. At least one child that I know of."

Markeem slumped in his chair.

"You cursed me in public," he said. "Screaming and crying."

"The grief was real. The anger was real. I just played it up to keep her safe—to stop you from looking."

"Why tell me now? After all these years?"

"So you can forgive yourself. You're the only one in this story who's allowed to." She stared him down, and for a moment she looked sober. "Also, I'll turn you in if you go looking for her. I have that leverage now. The dagger tattoo on your hand, the burn scars on your arms." She was looking him over as if cataloging new details. "Then I'll pick up the phone and say: 'I think I recognized his voice, Chief Mills.'"

He found a stack of clean shop rags in a cardboard box and wiped his eyes.

He didn't know what to say or how to feel.

Valerie stepped outside, sucking on the last half-inch of her cigarette. She looked smaller, slightly haunted. Like a fortune-teller on a smoke break.

"I'll let you pack," she said. "Looks like I caught you just in time."

"What about you?"

"What about me?"

"Where will you go?"

She crushed her cigarette and tracked an airplane that was veering north over the Santa Cruz Mountains, sunlight sparking off the passenger windows as it pitched high above her. She watched it very intently, as if expecting to find something there. Something promised, something dreamed of. She made a little gesture at the sky, then withdrew her hand.

"Nowhere," she said, her bloodshot eyes starting to flow. "Nowhere fast."

***

He waited three years before searching.

It was Thanksgiving and the bar was full of lonely, sentimental drunks. Someone brought a bone-dry turkey with mashed potatoes, and they all sat at the bar and ate quietly with gravy pooled in their plates, glancing up at the football game. When the last of them staggered back to their empty trailers along the slough, Markeem sat in the corner of the bar with his laptop and a pint of lager and he combed the Internet for traces of Jenna. The first thing he found was Valerie's obituary. It was recent, and devastatingly brief. It said that Jenna had predeceased her. He searched Valerie's socials for relatives, and by the time he'd finished his pint, he found a niece in Milwaukee with a connection named Jenna Jacobs. The profile picture was a mid-thirties blonde with a laughing child in her arms. It looked like she'd had the tattoo of the dripping syringe removed from her left hand. He stared at the photo a long while. Maybe they were at a park or in the woods somewhere outside of town. That big smile. Laugh lines. A hint of crows' feet creeping along her temples.

He shut the laptop and watched the coastal fog looming in the window.

He thought she'd be a teenage junkie forever.

She was never supposed to grow old.

He thought of Valerie, too. Not with pity or blame, but with a spark of appreciation for what she'd sacrificed for her daughter. She'd kept Jenna's secret as long as she needed to, and when the time came, she killed the man who'd given her so many secrets to keep.

His cell phone rang.

"Working late?" said the voice. "There's still pie if you're hungry."

"I was just closing up," said Markeem. "Ten minutes."

"Could you pick up a few jars of baby food on the way? That little pharmacy might be open."

"Of course," he said. He clicked on his own profile picture and noticed the lines on his face, the baby squealing in his arms. He waited a moment with the phone pressed to his ear, not even sure she was still on the line. "I love you, sugar."

"Love you, too. Hurry back home, okay?"

Paloma

With a few seconds left until the lunch break, Jeanie Kurcik wanders to the back of the classroom and kneels at the desk of Paloma Russell, a small and quiet girl with wild brown hair and mismatched clothing.

"Stay for a minute," she says, in a gentle voice.

The bell rings. The girl stares at her hands while the other students tumble from their desks and spill into the hallway, kicking their backpacks along the newly waxed floor as they go. It's a sunny day and everyone wants to be outside. Jeanie hauls a school desk from the row and spins it so she can sit facing the girl at her level.

"You're not in trouble," says Jeanie. "Not even a little."

The girl glances up, then back to her hands.

"I noticed you've been quiet lately," says Jeanie. "Usually, you have a lot to say when we talk about pre-Columbian history. Everything okay?"

"Sure," says the girl, almost a whisper.

"It's okay to feel like things *aren't okay*. Does that make sense?"

"Sort of. I guess."

"You know," says Jeanie—and she says this part carefully, "I was up on West Cliff Drive last night, by the lighthouse. I saw you eating dinner in a van with your father. A blue van. Looked like you'd been parked there awhile."

The girl tries not to cry.

"Can I go to the cafeteria now?" she asks. "I'm hungry."

"Of course you can," says Jeanie. "You're completely free to go." She steps out of the desk and nods at the door. "The thing is, I have a secret I wanted to share with you. Do you want to know what it is before you go?"

Paloma flicks her hair from her eyes, shoulders into her backpack. Some of the tears she's been holding run down her nose and gather there without falling.

"What is it?"

"That's where I live, too," says Jeanie.

"You sleep at the lighthouse?"

"Yes, sometimes."

"You're a teacher."

"I know. But that's how I saw you last night. I don't have my apartment anymore, so I park my minivan there to sleep the night. Either there, or down by Costco, but I don't like that area as much."

"I don't like that area either," says Paloma. "Too many people creeping around. Sometimes they bother us and won't go away. There's a man that keeps yelling at my daddy, being mean."

"Has he ever hurt your daddy?"

The girl gives a quick nod. "Once, real bad."

"Has he ever hurt you?"

"Not yet."

"Well, that's what I wanted to tell you. If you don't feel safe, just know that I might be parked nearby. And if you see me, it's okay to come say hi, got it? I don't want you to feel like you and your father are the only ones in your situation. Because you're most definitely not. There's lots of us."

Jeanie holds out her hand, and when she opens it, there's a silver whistle on a chain resting in the well of her palm.

"Take it," says Jeanie. "If I hear it, I'll know you need help. All you need to do is get a little air in your lungs and let it sing. And if I don't hear it, someone else will."

When the girl looks up, Jeanie sees that her expression has changed. It goes from shock to something like relief. She takes the silver whistle and shoves it into her pocket like a lucky talisman and scampers to the door. On her way out, she turns and smiles, and then she is gone.

***

Jeanie's crossing the fitness center parking lot with her gym bag over her shoulder when Ron Cash from the Cash Collection Agency calls. He's called so many times this year that she's added him as a contact in her phone. His voicemails were always robotic—*Ms. Kurcik, I'm calling about the eighteen-thousand seven hundred and forty-nine dollars in privately-held student loans*—but she finds him oddly polite and sympathetic whenever she answers. She thinks sometimes he calls just to talk to her, to see how she's getting along. A slight infatuation, perhaps.

"It's not a good time, Ron," she says. "I'm about to get on the road."

"On the road, huh?" He sounds even friendlier than usual, maybe a little drunk. "Going anywhere interesting?"

"If you consider the laundromat interesting."

"I'm from Nebraska. You'd be surprised what we find interesting out here. A three-legged cow came down the center of town last month and everyone's still talking about it." He chuckles—he really does find it funny.

"Now that is interesting," says Jeanie. "But really—"

"I know, I know. I'll get out of your hair. I just need to ask you on the record if you're in a position to begin payments on this debt. Even fifty dollars a month to start. We can accommodate just about any situation."

"I just started a GoFundMe site for classroom supplies. I can't even afford crayons. You start donating to my site, and we'll talk."

"I see it here," says Ron. "*Help Jeanie Kurcik's Third Grade Class*. Just sent five dollars your way. Five dollars is still worth something in Nebraska, though maybe it doesn't go as far out in California. Would ten be better? Not much, I know, but I hope it helps."

"It all adds up," says Jeanie, even though it's a lie.

It's the same lie she tells the kids during the magazine drive and the fall bake sale. Truth is, *it never adds up to anything*. Debts grow deeper, rents slip further out of reach. Next thing you know, you're exchanging a studio apartment for a sun-faded Dodge Caravan with missing hubcaps and illegal tinting—but hey, at least it's a coastal town and the views from the top of the parking garage aren't bad. Then someone starts a war and the price of gasoline doubles. Dime stores become dollar stores—and soon those become vintage boutiques for college kids with rich parents and Cadillac health care plans.

Maybe it adds up for some people.

Maybe it subtracts from everyone else.

"Why don't I check in next week?" says Ron. "Maybe your luck will change."

"Sure," says Jeanie. "I'll go buy a lottery ticket."

***

'They didn't have homelessness in pre-Columbian times because Native people took care of each other. They lived in large extended families and shared their food and their homes. It didn't matter if you were sick or old. They would take care of you anyways. I think we should try this idea so people don't go homeless and get sick in the street.'

Jeanie sits at a small table in the corner of the laundromat, looking over Paloma Russell's social studies assignment. She reads it twice through, then pauses to watch the evening traffic on Laurel Street. A lone pedestrian threads the slow-moving cars toward the park on the corner. Someone has pitched a ragged nylon tent by the drinking fountain and a park ranger is yelling and gesturing at it with the butt of his flashlight. She can't quite hear what he's saying over the sounds of the washing machines and the cars idling on the road.

"All we have are these little creamer packets," says Carla, the barista who runs the laundromat coffee cart. She's a large woman with thinning gray hair and a bluish tattoo of a sparrow on her chest. She wears long earrings made of brightly colored plastic beads that look homemade. She comes limping across the room and settles a cup and saucer amid the stacks of papers on Jeanie's table. "The fresh creamer went bad. Guess it wasn't so fresh after all."

"These little creamers are fine," says Jeanie. "Thank you."

"You crying?" she asks, with a tilt of her head, earrings jangling.

Jeanie gestures at the stack of papers. "Sometimes a student will write something and it hits close to home."

Carla nods as if she understands this well.

"Boy, ain't it the truth," she says. "My kids would say all sorts of things that cut to the quick. Not to be mean or nothing—they just noticed things and didn't know what should be said and what shouldn't. No filter, I guess."

"Seems like we spend our whole lives being told not to notice things."

"Squeaky wheels don't get the grease anymore," says Carla. "They get tossed in the trash, replaced with cheaper plastic wheels. What's the point?"

"Your kids still live around here?"

"My son does. Took me to the hospital last week but it turned into a disaster."

"I saw you were limping," says Jeanie. "Something happen to your leg?"

"They think it's the diabetes," she says, pointing to her swollen left calf. "My son dragged me to the ER even though it meant blowing off my night shift at the ARCO station. But wouldn't you know it, some city cop recognized my son and said he had a warrant for his arrest. Next thing you know, they're cuffing him up and hauling him off to jail. Right there in the waiting room. Boy, I was hopping mad. Damn near got myself arrested alongside him."

"That's awful," says Jeanie. "You'd think the ER would be off limits."

"You'd think—but no ma'am."

"I can take you, if you want. What time does your shift end?"

Carla huffed as she backed away. "You're sweet. But my shift don't ever end, girlie. It rolls straight into the next one. And the one after that. Besides, I ain't ever going back to that damn hospital. I'd cut off my own leg if I had to. Right off at the knee."

"I'll leave my number," says Jeanie. "There's more than one hospital in the county in case you change your mind. I let a major health issue go unchecked a few years back and it took me a long time to recover. Still haven't, to be honest. I don't want to see it happen to anyone else."

"You're sweet," she says again. "Maybe I'll take you up on it."

Jeanie takes a sip of coffee and settles back over her school papers. She reads Paloma's assignment a third time and again her eyes drift out the window toward the park. A pair of city cops have joined the park ranger, encircling an old man with a filthy blanket draped over his shoulders. They're asking him questions, gesturing at the tent. He shakes his head with his palms pressed together. Jeanie can read the words on his lips: *no sir, no sir, no sir, please sir.*

***

With the laundry folded and assignments graded, she heads up West Cliff Drive toward the lighthouse, the smell of clean clothes brightening the old van funk. By now, the sun has set. All that remains is a rusty bar of light that stretches low over the Monterey Bay and out toward the Pacific. She looks for the girl. At first pass, she can't catch any sight of her, or her father's blue van. She circles again. Most of the overnighters have claimed their spots for the evening and there aren't many spaces left. A few joggers shuffle along the cliff. A spandexed man on a recumbent bike zips low and nimble like a centipede. An older couple strolls with a little white dog on a glittery leash. Jeanie finds a spot along the cliff and sits idling, looking out over the bay. Little whitecaps surging and fading in the dark. She worries she'd given Paloma too many assurances, that maybe she'd been unrealistic with her. It was hard enough finding a place to park that wouldn't draw the ire of law enforcement, let alone a spot to watch over the girl. Still, she can't stop worrying about her. She thinks she hears the sound of a whistle blowing, but it's only the seawind catching the radio antennae, making it sing.

***

It's eight o'clock when Jeanie reaches the Costco on Sylvania Avenue. The street is busier than she remembers. Lone figures shuffle through the headlights, faces hard and secretive. The twang of a country song blares over a cheap car stereo. She spots the blue van under a redwood tree with a subtle orange lantern glow in the windows. She parks and waits. Her legs are sore and trembling from cross-training at the gym. There's a bunch of half-ripe bananas in a makeshift pantry on the passenger floorboard and she opens it and sits eating and watching. She thinks she can see Paloma's face caught in the blue glow of a phone or tablet as if she's looking through an airplane window at some distant skyline.

Around midnight, she wakes to the sound of yelling and pounding, and at first Jeanie can't tell if she'd yelled in her sleep or if it's coming from the street. The headlights have all gone dark, radios quiet. She sees a bald man with a beard standing by the blue van, banging his fists on the front quarter panel. He's yelling *open up*, and Paloma's father is yelling *fuck off*.

Jeanie straightens in her seat.

The bald man quits his tirade and limps into the shadows of the redwood tree, and when he reappears, he's hauling a chunk of concrete on his shoulder like some deranged prison laborer. He raises it up over his head to smash the windshield, but the door slides open and Paloma's father appears, showing his hands. They curse each other, the bald man demanding either *ten grand* or *ten grams*—Jeanie can't tell which. Then the bald man dumps the chunk of concrete into the street, takes Paloma's father by the shirt collar, and headbutts him in the nose.

Jeanie can hear Paloma screaming from inside the van, and she watches as the girl's father buckles and topples to the ground. She launches the call app on her phone and dials 911. As it's ringing, the man kneels over Paloma's father and beats him as he lay in the street. The blows sound awful and wet, like a child stomping a puddle.

"Hey," says Jeanie. She slips out of the van and inches toward them with her phone held out. "Leave them alone. The police are on their way."

The bald man doesn't hear her at first, so she says it again, louder.

The dispatcher picks up, asking questions.

"Someone's getting beat up behind the Costco on Sylvania Avenue," says Jeanie, into the phone. "There's a bald man with a dark brown beard and a tattoo on his left cheek. *Please hurry.*"

The bald man rises.

"Who the fuck are you?" he says—sort of a bewildered murmur, as if she'd broken some inviolable code of the street. He has this fiendish look about him—a man fully consumed by violence. Jaw set, eyes darkly fuming like iron slag. Even in the dim light of the streetlamp she can see the blood on his knuckles, the spatter on his forehead.

Jeanie backpedals, and the man starts after her. He lopes crookedly with something held low at his side, something he doesn't want anyone to see. She fumbles for the door handle, dropping her phone on the asphalt, the dispatcher's tin voice chattering at her feet. There is some comfort knowing that if he catches her, if he really starts beating her up, at least the dispatcher will hear it and somehow hasten the response. She barely gets the door open when the street brightens, and the man's face fills with light.

One by one, the parked cars and vans flick on their headlights and sound their horns. The honking swells. Some people are climbing out in their pajamas, phones held high as if recording the scene. Flashlights beaming. The street is crowded again, and the thought occurs to Jeanie that maybe it's the man who has now broken the unwritten rules of the street. It's as if Jeanie and the bald man are street actors, spotlit before an audience, about to close out a scene.

The bald man withdraws.

He stoves his hands in his pockets and slinks under the redwood tree.

One by one headlights dim and the horns fall silent.

Jeanie runs to the girl.

****

Next day, Paloma is absent.

From school records, Jeanie learns the father's name is Roger Russell, and she spends the lunch hour calling the local hospitals trying to find him. After the assault, he'd regained consciousness and driven off erratically with Paloma in the backseat before the police could respond. She'd only had a moment to speak to the girl, just enough to see her with the silver whistle dangling from her hand, too scared to cry.

"I'm sorry," she had said, gesturing to her throat, the words hardly coming out. "I couldn't blow the whistle. I couldn't even breathe."

"It's okay," Jeanie had said. "Nothing was your fault—just take it slow. You'll find your voice. And when you do, nobody will ever take it away from you."

She gets the report number from the police department and files her own report with Child Protective Services, but without an address and a current phone number, Paloma Russell is in the wind. She learns from asking around that the bald man's name is Cyrus. Nobody knows his last name, or where he camps—only that he's a known menace, a spook story. There is something about his name that makes everyone whisper and shift their eyes when it is spoken.

She drives all over town looking for the blue van, without luck. She checks all the usual places. Sometime after dark, after showering at the gym and a few handfuls of trail mix, she dials Ron Cash's number. He answers the phone after the third ring.

"It's me," says Jeanie. "Jeanie Kurcik from California."

He sounds happy. "Didn't think I'd hear your voice till next week. You ready to start repayment? Kinda late in the evening ain't it?"

"I need a favor, Ron. One of my students is in trouble."

He makes a confused sound—a drawn-out questioning sound.

"Is this about your GoFundMe page?" he says, finally.

"No. It's about a young girl in a lot of danger. Can you look up police records?"

"Not in the way I think you mean, no. But as long as it's a public record, I can run a decent query. You'd be surprised how much information is public, long as you have the right subscriptions. Everything okay?"

"No, Ron. Everything's not okay. But I promise to start paying on the loan tomorrow if you do me this one big favor. I need you to look up arrest records in my town for a man named Cyrus. I don't know his last name. Anything recent will do. He's a thirty-something white guy with a tattoo of a spider web on his cheek. Can you do that?"

"Well, let me see. Gonna pour myself another whiskey first."

"Did you hear the description?"

"Cyrus. White guy. Spider web. Got it."

He takes a noisy sip and says *ah*. He's a loud typer and she can hear him hammering the keys like some old-school newspaper reporter on a deadline. He maunders to himself for a minute or two, then gradually his maundering takes a positive tone.

"Cyrus Erwood," he says. "I'm looking at a booking photo right now. Bald guy with a spider web tattoo. Looks like a real tough son of a bitch."

"How tough?" says Jeanie. "What's he been booked for?"

"Well, I'm no expert on violation codes. But I think a 459 is a burglary. There's maybe some drug stuff here, too." The keyboard strokes grow louder, more precise. "Hold on, let me look this up. Okay, looks like a bunch of assault and weapons charges a couple years back. Sex crimes, too. It's a wonder they let a guy like this back on the streets. You said he had something to do with a student of yours?"

Jeanie slips into the driver seat and starts the ignition.

"Can you text me the latest booking photo?" she says.

"Sure, I can do that. But you're not gonna get tangled up with this guy, are you Jeanie? He looks dangerous. I know he is, based on his booking records. Even his name sounds dangerous."

"Don't worry—this time tomorrow we'll be setting up a payment plan together. You'll finally get a piece of me, Ron. Just as long as you send me that photo."

"It's not about the money," he says. "I know it seems that way, but—"

"What country are you living in? It's always about the fucking money."

***

The unhoused residents of Sylvania Avenue don't want to talk. Most of the folks at the lighthouse are tightlipped too, though she finds a man who claims he's seen Cyrus Erwood driving a Nissan pickup with a white camper shell recently.

"He keeps track of everybody," says the man. He's an old man with a long white beard and tobacco stains in his wiry mustache who'd been kind to Jeanie when she first lost her apartment. "Some say he's the devil, with eyes and ears all over town. If you owe him a debt, he's always on your heels. Tell you what—if I had a choice, I'd sooner owe the devil than Mr. Erwood."

She keeps searching. Under the redwood trestle at Beach Hill, Jeanie approaches a young woman sitting cross-legged on a mosaic of flattened cardboard boxes with a smoldering campfire nearby. She glances at the booking photo and shrinks away with her eyes shut tight.

"Get it away from me," says the woman. "I can't look at him."

Jeanie clicks off her phone and clutches it to her chest.

"You know him?" she asks, but the woman falls silent. "I think he might lead me to a girl, a student of mine. She's in a lot of trouble."

"You're a teacher?"

"Yes. Third grade. Bay View Elementary."

The woman considers this, sitting back on her hands. A cold sea-wind blows through the crossbeams of the old trestle and a lone dove claps off into the eucalyptus trees. She draws a blanket over her shoulders and stares off toward the Municipal Wharf where cars line up at the little kiosk to pay their parking fees.

"I saw a girl in a blue van the other night, down by Costco. She waved at me and I waved back. Looked like a third grader."

"That's her," says Jeanie. "Her name's Paloma. This Erwood guy assaulted her father and now she's not showing up at school. I'm afraid for her. And I know she's afraid, too."

"Does he owe Cyrus money, the father?"

"I believe he does."

The woman produces a vape pen and draws on it. Her face lights up with an eerie LED glow and a thick white vapor billows over her lap like dry ice.

"You should try Chestnut Street, behind the Mexican Market," says the woman. "I've seen Cyrus park there a bunch of times. His face haunts me. I can see it when I close my eyes and all I want to do is erase it forever. I just want to think about good things from now on, but it seems like all the things I want to forget only get bolder, while all my favorite memories fade away."

"I won't bother you again," says Jeanie. She fishes a twenty-dollar-bill from her front pocket and hands it to the woman. "For your trouble. Get yourself something to eat."

The woman takes the twenty and studies it against the light of a streetlamp.

"Wish I had a teacher like you when I was a kid," she says. "Nobody ever gave a shit about me. It gives me a little hope."

***

The Mexican market is only a mile from the trestle. Jeanie parks on the street a half block away and surveys the parking lot with a pair of thrift store binoculars. There are a few cars behind the market that look lived in. A minivan, a Chevy Tahoe, an old RV with a massive tear in the side. Behind the RV, she can just make out the tailgate of a Nissan pickup with a dented rear bumper and a camper attached. She waits, listening to the radio. Some NPR segment about sea urchins. After an hour, the camper window swings open, and the tailgate drops. Cyrus Erwood slides his short legs out and hops onto the asphalt with a lit cigarette or joint in his mouth. He takes a few drags, unpockets a cell phone, and begins working the screen with his thumbs like a spider kneading a web, little puffs of smoke trailing as he paces the lot. After a few minutes, he buttons up the camper window and backs the truck out of the space and onto the road.

Jeanie follows.

They pass the laundromat on Laurel Street, then across Pacific Avenue with its mix of tourists, college students, and panhandlers—all shuffling toward the center of town or retreating from it. They cross the San Lorenzo River, where the homeless camp along the weedy banks in dense coyote brush, making secret fires in the gathering fog. She follows him down Ocean View Avenue toward the little sloping park that overlooks the lower half of the city. She's already flicked off her headlights, and now she gives some distance. Roger Russell's blue van sits beside a fire hydrant with a parking ticket on the windshield. Cyrus approaches it on foot, peering in the dark windows with his hands cupped against the glass.

Jeanie watches as Cyrus places a call on his cell, hands jerking while he talks. He's yelling about all his *fucking money* and where it went. Then he abruptly turns and limps into the park toward the overlook. Jeanie slips a crowbar from under her seat and follows on foot. She pauses at Roger Russell's van and places her palm on the hood, looks through the windshield. The hood is cold—no sign of the girl. She can see Cyrus's silhouette hurrying toward the other end of the park, his form stamped against the far-off lights of the Beach Boardwalk. The night is very still, and she can hear the distant ride cars zipping along the old wooden tracks of the Giant Dipper, the screams reaching faintly across the river.

She creeps through the dark of the trees and along an old fence strangled with ivy. She follows him down a dirt path and soon she can make out a campsite nestled among the cedar trees, a small campfire crackling and smoking. There are several paper bags circling the camp, and two lawn chairs are set up near the fire. Roger Russell sits in one of the chairs, gazing up at the starless sky. Sitting by the paper bags, she spots Paloma with a blanket cinched around her shoulders, wild hair shrouding her face like some dust bowl refugee.

The girl draws the blanket tight when Cyrus appears.

Jeanie shuffles quickly behind him.

"Leave them alone," she says, and Cyrus wheels around.

"You again," he says. He stands so he can keep Roger Russell and Jeanie in his periphery. But his attention soon fixes on Roger, who hasn't budged. He sits motionless in his chair—crooked nose, swollen lips, black eyes. Cyrus nudges him with the heel of his boot, and he tips over and falls stiffly into the dirt. A horde of ants teem from the cuff of his pants as he falls.

Paloma whimpers. "*Oh daddy!*"

"Now here's a man who can't take a punch," says Cyrus. He has the macabre interest of a boy finding a dead animal. "Maybe I broke something loose in that little brain of his. Question is—which one of these bags has the money he took from me? You gonna help me look, little girl?"

"Paloma, come with me," says Jeanie. "Don't answer him."

The girl rises and hurries across the camp, but Cyrus catches her by the wrist.

"No you don't, sugar. You ain't going nowhere till Uncle Cyrus gets his money."

"Let her go," Jeanie shouts, choking up on the tire iron. "Don't you fucking touch her."

"You her grandma or something?" says Cyrus, pulling the girl close, his spidery fingers curling over her shoulders. Paloma looks as if she's hyperventilating. "You can have her for ten grand. Sound like a fair trade, Grandma? I'm not supposed to be around children anyway."

She unlocks her phone and dials 911.

"Paloma, honey, the police are on their way. It'll be over real soon—"

"It'll be over when I get my money," says Cyrus, and he lets go of the girl and charges Jeanie, driving her back against a tree trunk. He presses into her, growling into her ear. "One thing I can't stand is a busy body. All you old ladies getting in the middle of everyone's business, thinking the world belongs to you. It's my world, okay? I say who stays in it and who has to leave. You had your turn."

He'd pinned the phone between them, but her other arm still hangs free, so she jabs the spear of the tire iron into his ear. It's the first time she's ever hurt anyone and there's a part of her that wants to make sure he isn't hurt too bad. He jerks away, eyes fluttering, jaw sliding back and forth, exposing those rotten black teeth. His brain can't seem to process what happened. She spots a four-inch knife dangling from his tattooed fingers, fresh blood gathered on the steel.

His face is sinister and contorted.

He raises the knife.

Jeanie swings again, this time hitting him flat across the forehead. He stumbles back a few steps, trips over Roger Russell's corpse, and topples into the campfire, sending a helix of bright orange sparks into the tree canopy. He makes no effort to roll to safety—just lies there, fleshy pink face searing and smoking in the coals.

Jeanie takes a step toward the girl, but her legs buckle.

The pain from the knife wound catches her all at once. Blood curtains down her legs. She drops to her knees looking for the phone. She'd already dialed the number. All she has to do is find it and talk. She asks the girl for help, but she only stands there, tears streaming, choking on her breath.

"Breathe," says Jeanie, elbowing back into the cold grass. Somewhere a dispatcher prattles from the lost phone. "I know you're scared. It's okay to be scared. You'll find your voice again if you just breathe."

The fog thins. An orange moon rises over the amusement park across the river. The park-goers' screams come and go as ride cars bolt around the hairpin turns. Seabirds drift through the sky—Jeanie thinks she can hear them calling to each other, their shrieks wind-dampened, soft as cricketsong.

The birds vanish and Paloma appears above her with the whistle at her lips, louder than the sizzle of the fire, louder than the roller coaster cars. She has found her breath at last, and she blows the whistle as if no one will ever take it away from her. Windows brighten in the nearby houses. Dark figures peer through the glass with phones glowing in their hands.

Jeanie's breath quickens and her legs turn cold. She closes her eyes, and the night grows heavy and still. She can barely hear the whistle anymore—not much louder than a bird's shriek, or the distant howls of sirens, or sea wind through a radio antenna, or a lone dove clapping off into a eucalyptus tree. Yet Jeanie knows the whistle is still loud enough to matter.

ACKNOWLEDGEMENTS:

I want to thank my publisher, **Rock and a Hard Place Press,** for the opportunity to present this work, and whose every publication feels like a righteous act of rebellion in an increasingly hostile world. Especially Paul Garth, whose immense talents made this collection the best it could be. Also Roger Nokes, Jay Butkowski, and Rob Smith—you've always been a pleasure to work with. I want to thank M.E. Proctor, Coy Hall, Jeff Esterholm, James D.F. Hannah, Meagan Lucas, Wes Browne, and Nikki Dolson for their advance praise of the book and continued support of my writing. I also want to thank S.A. Cosby, who despite his mythic stature in the crime fiction world, gave a small-time writer a piece of advice that still keeps me motivated. Others I want to mention: Holly West, Frank Vatel, Victor de Anda, Susan Jesen, Curtis Ippolito, Zakariah Johnson, Jeff Circle, Kirstyn Petras, and Nathan Turner. I especially want to thank my family: my mom, Debra, for her eternal encouragement, and for buying everything I've ever written (maybe two of everything), my father, Rick, my two sons, Enzo and Miles, and my wife, Amy Rose, for always championing my writing and putting up with my late nights of clacking on the keyboard in the dark.

ABOUT THE AUTHOR:

C.W. **Blackwell** is an American author from the Central Coast of California. His short stories have appeared with Down and Out Books, *Mystery Magazine*, *Shotgun Honey*, *Tough Magazine*, and *Reckon Review*. He is a 2x Derringer Award winner and 4x nominee. He won the SuRaa Fiction Award in 2022 and was included as a Distinguished Author in the *2024 Best American Mystery and Suspense* collection. His folk horror novella *Song of the Red Squire* was published in 2022 from Nosetouch Press. His crime fiction novella *Hard Mountain Clay* was published in January 2023 from Shotgun Honey Books.

9 7 9 8 9 9 1 2 9 5 0 7 9